W9-DGB-515

RACHEL TAKES THE LEAD

RACHEL TAKES THE LEAD

Marilyn Kaye

HOLIDAY HOUSE is registered in the U.S. Patent and Trademark Office.
Printed and bound in May 2021 at Maple Press, York, PA, USA.
www.holidayhouse.com
First Edition
1 3 5 7 9 10 8 6 4 2

Library of Congress Cataloging-in-Publication Data
Names: Kaye, Marilyn, author.
Title: Rachel takes the lead / by Marilyn Kaye.
Description: First edition. | New York : Holiday House, [2021] | Series: The spyglass sisterhood ; #2 | Audience: Ages 8–12. | Audience: Grades 4–6. | Summary: Twelve-year-old Rachel, who is very shy, gets help from friends Ellie, Alyssa, and Kiara to run for seventh-grade class representative and to seek the owner of a dog she found.
Identifiers: LCCN 2020051040 (print) | LCCN 2020051041 (ebook)
ISBN 9780823446100 (hardcover) | ISBN 9780823448999 (ebook)
Subjects: CYAC: Bashfulness—Fiction. | Friendship—Fiction.
Elections—Fiction. | Middle schools—Fiction. | Schools—Fiction.
Lesbian mothers—Fiction. | Magic—Fiction. | Telescopes—Fiction.
Classification: LCC PZ7.K2127 Rac 2021 (print) | LCC PZ7.K2127 (ebook)
DDC [Fic]—dc23
LC record available at https://lccn.loc.gov/2020051040
LC ebook record available at https://lccn.loc.gov/2020051041

ISBN: 978-0-8234-4610-0 (hardcover)

For Rose Loiseau, with love from her godmother

chapter one

HELLO. MY NAME IS RACHEL LEVIN-LOPEZ, AND I have to tell you right off that I really don't want to be doing this. I'm supposed to introduce myself to you, but the thing is, I'm shy. Very shy. I don't like talking about myself, and I don't think *writing* about myself is going to be any easier for me. But since I'm the one telling this story, you readers deserve to know who I am. So I'll try.

I'll start with the easy stuff. I'm twelve years old, and I'm in the seventh grade at East Lakeside Middle School. I'm short, and I have long, curly blond hair that can get very frizzy, depending on the weather.

I'm pale, and I blush a lot, which turns me pink. Sometimes even red. I live in a small, pretty house with my parents: Jane Levin-Lopez, who I call Mom, and Cecilia Levin-Lopez, otherwise known to me as Mami. Mami was born in Mexico and that's how you say *Mom* in Spanish. Mami teaches Spanish at Lakeside High School, and Mom is a graphic designer who works mostly at home. I love them both and they love me. Maybe a little too much.

Now I'll get to the not-so-easy stuff. My parents are what you might call overprotective. They don't want me to be out alone—they want to go with me everywhere I go, or at least get me there and pick me up. Mom even walks me to and from school, as if I was a little kid. It's kind of embarrassing, at my age, but I guess I can understand why they do this.

You see, before I was born, they had another child. Her name was Leah, and when she was ten years old, she was hit by a car while walking home from school by herself. And she died. Mom and Mami don't talk about this much, but there's a framed photograph of Leah on the mantel over the fireplace. Every now and then, when one of them looks at it, I can see the sadness in her face. And because of this tragedy, one or the other or both of them want to be by my side, watching over me, protecting me from any possible dangers. All the time.

So I'm an only child. Growing up, I wasn't ever really sad about that. I've always been good at keeping myself busy. I read a lot, and I like to write down ideas for stories and poems. I haven't actually *written* any stories or poems, but I think someday I will. And I keep a diary, which I don't show to anyone. But I have to admit that sometimes I've been lonely. When you're as shy as I am, it's not easy making friends.

Then, almost two months ago, in January, all that changed.

It began when Ellie Marks arrived in Lakeside. Her family moved into an old Victorian house, complete with a turret on top, and it was up there that Ellie discovered an old telescope bolted to the floor. She soon realized that this was no ordinary telescope. Looking through it for the first time, she saw our entire town, including a community center with a swimming pool. Which seemed normal, except later that day, she learned that the community center didn't exist. The citizens of Lakeside *wanted* a community center, but it hadn't been built yet. Pretty weird, right?

At first, Ellie thought the telescope could show her the future. Which would be cool enough—but it turned out there were more surprises to come.

Those surprises began when she peered through the telescope again and saw our classmate, Alyssa

Parker, sitting on a broomstick, flying over Lakeside. Of course, that wasn't something that could ever happen—not then, and not in the future. But Ellie was curious about what the vision might mean, so she got to know Alyssa and found out that she sometimes *daydreamed* of being a witch. Mainly so she could put curses on people she didn't like. Of course, when Ellie told Alyssa what she'd seen, Alyssa was curious, so Alyssa and Ellie started looking through the telescope together.

Next, Alyssa and Ellie saw me, walking with Mom—only in this telescope vision, I looked like I was about five years old. When they cornered me in the school cafeteria to ask me about what they'd seen, I confessed that five years old was exactly how I felt sometimes because of the way my parents treat me. After that, I was invited to look through the telescope with them.

It wasn't long before Ellie, Alyssa, and I saw another classmate through the lens: Kiara Douglas, running around in the playground with oversized cartoon animals. Eventually, we learned that Kiara was hooked on playing this online game where all the characters are animals. It turned out that her fellow players were her only friends. She didn't even know who they really were, since they used avatars with made-up names. Since Kiara wasn't exactly an outgoing person, it took some effort to connect with her, but she eventually decided to join us too.

So the telescope wasn't just showing the future. It was showing us *feelings*—what people wanted, their fantasies, and maybe their fears too. This realization was pretty exciting. But what was even more exciting, for me, was that this telescope brought us together. We started calling it a spyglass, which sounded more magical to us, and we decided to call ourselves the Spyglass Sisterhood. We vowed not to tell anyone else about what the spyglass could do, not even our families, for two reasons. First of all, no one would believe us. And second, because even if they *did* believe us, they'd all want to look in the spyglass and it would become famous and someone would take it away from us.

Having friends is a big change for me. One thing I learned really fast is that being friends doesn't mean we're alike. The word *sisterhood* might make you think we have a lot in common, but that's not true at all. In our looks, our home lives, our personalities, in just about every possible way, we're very different.

Alyssa is tall and thin. She has long, straight black hair and a golden-tan complexion. She's into the goth look and wears black makeup and clothes all the time. And she's dark in other ways too. She doesn't smile a lot, she's sarcastic, and she acts unfriendly to most people. I think she does this mainly to annoy her family. But with us, the sisterhood, she's cool.

She lives in a big, modern house that was designed by her stepfather, who's an architect. Her mother is a very important surgeon. Alyssa calls her "Dr. Gina Khatri, cardiac catheter wizard to the stars." Alyssa has a nine-year-old brother who's already a talented actor. She has an older stepbrother who's a big deal at Lakeside High—an athlete, president of the student body, and smart too. And an older stepsister, a figure skater who's training for the Olympics. Personally, I think Alyssa's style and attitude are her way of standing out in this family of big shots.

Kiara is tiny, as short as I am, but much thinner. She's Black, and she wears her hair in an elaborate cornrow design that looks like she's wearing a beautiful tiara when she pins it up. Her mother died when she was a baby, and she's an only child like me. She lives in a fancy apartment with her father, who's a professor of history at Bascomb College here in Lakeside.

I guess you could say Kiara has kind of a quirky personality. At first, we thought she was snobbish, because she resisted our attempts to bring her into the sisterhood. But friendship's not something you can push. Especially with someone like Kiara, who's just not a very sociable person by nature. With us, she says exactly what she thinks, and sometimes that hurts, but unlike Alyssa, she isn't rude on purpose. It's just the way she is. She's totally honest and very intelligent. She has an amazing vocabulary and she's a science and math whiz. As far as style goes, she's not particularly interested in fashion. She's always neatly dressed, but that's about it. She probably wouldn't even have her cool hairstyle if her aunt wasn't a hairdresser.

I suppose Ellie could be called the leader of our group. She brought us all together, she has the spyglass, and we hang out at her house. She definitely likes to take charge. And even though I don't want to say anything negative about my friends, Ellie can be a little bossy sometimes.

She has an older sister who's away at college, so we haven't met her yet. Her mother's a newspaper reporter, and her father's a lawyer. He works from an office in their house, which makes my parents happy since they know there's always an adult around. What's really nice about Ellie's parents is that they don't mind that we're over there all the time. And even though they're both busy people, they still manage to keep the kitchen stocked with snacks for us.

Ellie's neither short nor tall, fat nor thin. She has brown hair, a medium complexion, and a few freckles. She calls herself ordinary, but I think that's only because she *used* to be. Before she moved to Lakeside, back at her old school, she was part of the popular crowd. She says she was a follower, she just blended in and did what everyone else did, until the day her parents got involved in a campaign to build a homeless shelter in their town. A lot of people were against the idea, and they turned their kids against Ellie. So when she came to Lakeside, Ellie was determined to have nothing to do with popular kids. Which is funny in a way, because she's actually friends with a popular kid here, Mike Twersky. She claims he's not her boyfriend, but I'm not sure I believe her.

Ellie's definitely not a follower anymore, but she still *looks* like she could be in the popular crowd, with her nice haircut and lip gloss. Her jeans are like theirs too—classic straight-leg ones, which she tops with cool sweaters in bright colors. I don't wear jeans or leggings—I prefer sweatpants and hoodies in the winter, little dresses in the spring and summer. At least my parents don't bug me about how I dress, the way Alyssa's mother does.

✦

Thinking about the sisterhood now, maybe we do have something in common. We're all pretty smart. Like I already said, Kiara is particularly good in science and math. I do very well in English. Ellie is above average in just about all subjects. Alyssa doesn't make perfect grades, but not because she isn't smart. She just doesn't try all that hard at school. I think maybe it's just another way for her to upset her outstanding family.

There's something else too. We're all loners. We don't fit into any of the cliques at school, and we don't try to. But we have different reasons for that. Ellie, because of her bad experience in her hometown. Me, because I'm shy. Kiara, because she prefers doing stuff on her own. Alyssa, because she says she's just not interested in most people. But we've got each other now, so I guess we're not really loners anymore.

You might be thinking I've told you more about my friends than I've told you about myself, and I guess you'd be right. It's funny, in a way...I think I probably know them better than they know me. And sometimes I wish I could be more like them. For example, I'd love to be as sure of myself as Alyssa (though not in the same way, since I don't want to wear skull earrings). Or maybe I could be more forward, the way Ellie is (though not as bossy). And I admire the way Kiara doesn't care what people think about her, and I wish I could be like that. And all three of them seem to have *so* much more confidence than I have.

Maybe that's why I don't open up very much to

them. Maybe because I never think I have anything interesting to say, and I always wait for them to start conversations. This is something I should probably work on.

Or maybe they don't know me very well because I don't really know myself. Does that make any sense?

Maybe if I knew myself better, they'd know me better. I think I need to work on that too.

chapter two

ON WEEKENDS, MAMI MAKES FABULOUS breakfasts. Everything from omelets to huevos rancheros to French toast covered in maple syrup—Mami can do it all. Visions of those meals danced in my head as I slowly woke up. For a brief moment, I thought I could even smell them.

But then I remembered that this was a Monday. And on Mondays, Mami always wants to be at the high school before seven o'clock, so there's no time for her to make a serious breakfast. And Mom, who has lots of other wonderful qualities, isn't much of a cook. She wants our food to be healthy and nutritious, but to be honest, she doesn't much care how it tastes.

So as I pulled on my robe and left my bedroom, no delicious aromas greeted me. In the kitchen, Mami was already dressed and finishing her coffee.

"Buenos días, mi hija," she sang out.

"Buenos días, Mami." I rubbed my eyes. "Mami, why do you always leave so early on Mondays?"

"Because, my darling daughter, as I've told you before, I do not like to work on weekends when I can spend time with my family. So I must get to school early to prepare my classes." She bent, kissed my forehead, and took one of her usual granola bars to eat on the way to work.

I grabbed a box of cereal. Mom, looking much less alert, came into the kitchen just as Mami was opening the back door.

"¡Adios!" Mami called, and blew us a kiss before she walked out.

Mom isn't a morning person. She mumbled a greeting, I greeted her back, and she began to rummage around in a cabinet for a mug. Back at the dining room table, she drank her coffee and I ate my cereal, and we sat in comfortable silence together.

By the time we left the house for the walk to my school, Mom could actually begin to talk like a human being.

"Anything special going on at school today?" she asked.

"Just the usual," I replied.

"No book reports to give?"

As much as I love to read, and to write about the books I read, I hate getting up in front of the class to present them. And this year, my English teacher has us doing a lot of presentations. Mom understands, and she's always prepared to give me a little pep talk when she knows I have to do it.

"Not today," I told her. "Oh, I'm going to Ellie's after school."

"And someone will give you a ride home? Or walk with you?"

She always asks that, and I sighed. *"Mom."* It's about a fifteen-minute walk from Ellie's house to mine, through a perfectly nice and safe neighborhood. And it was March, almost spring, so the sun wasn't going down as early as it was in January, when I first started going to Ellie's. I didn't bother pointing any of this out to Mom, though. Just like I didn't bother to respond to her question. She knew I would obey her wishes.

As usual, when we neared the school, I ducked my head so I wouldn't make eye contact with any classmates. Not that they'd notice me anyway. I'm always so quiet that nobody pays attention to me. But I still feel embarrassed about being walked to school.

I raised my eyes as we approached the entrance and was happy to see Alyssa and Kiara standing outside. I didn't have to be embarrassed in front of them.

"Hi, Ms. Levin-Lopez," they chorused politely, and Mom greeted them. She knew better than to kiss me publicly, so she just gave me a little squeeze on the shoulder and said, "Have a nice day, girls," before leaving.

"Hi," I said. "Where's Ellie?"

Alyssa looked to the right and then to the left. "Not here."

Kiara frowned. "I think that's obvious."

I grinned. This was so typical—Alyssa being a smart aleck and Kiara not recognizing her sarcasm.

"Okay," I said. "*Why* isn't she here?"

Neither of them knew, and then the warning bell rang. Everyone hanging out in front of the school started hurrying toward the building, and we did too. Since we all have different homerooms, we had to separate once we got inside.

There are about thirty kids in my homeroom, and as they entered, most of them stopped by friends' desks to talk before we all had to sit down. I didn't greet anyone, and no one greeted me. This was typical, and it didn't bother me at all. I slipped silently into my chair.

After a few minutes, people began going to their

assigned seats, except for Paige Nakamura and her little clique. Paige is practically famous in the seventh grade. To be perfectly honest, I've never really understood why kids look up to her, why they think she's so special. True, she's very pretty, she wears very nice clothes, and she carries handbags with the name of a designer on them. And she always wears a hairband that matches whatever else she's wearing. Lately, I've noticed that all her friends are wearing hairbands too. Paige is what you might call an influencer.

But she isn't a very nice person. I've heard her say pretty mean things to people. Alyssa told me that once, when Paige came into a classroom and saw Alyssa sitting at *her* desk, she accused Alyssa of spreading cooties.

There were just a few seconds before the final bell. Paige left her group and started walking in my direction. This made me nervous.

She paused by my desk and spoke loudly.

"I saw you coming to school," she said. "Was that your mother walking with you?"

Keeping my eyes fixed on my desk, I nodded. So much for going unnoticed this morning. Sometimes I wish I was really, truly invisible.

"I'm just curious," Paige continued. "Does she hold your hand when you cross a street?"

I heard a few giggles, and I could feel my face

getting warm. Then the bell rang, Paige went to her seat, and Mr. Greene came in.

"Good morning, everyone," he said. He opened a notebook on his desk and started calling roll.

I could feel my face growing hotter, and I knew it had to be turning red. Since I don't think much of Paige, I don't care what she thinks of me. But she's one of the most popular girls here, which means other kids pay attention to what she says. Would this mean the start of bullying for me?

"Rachel? Rachel Levin-Lopez?"

I looked up, startled. "Y-yes?"

"I'm only taking attendance," Mr. Greene said.

"Oh! Sorry. Here."

Behind me, I heard Paige whispering to the girl sitting next to her, and then the girl giggled. Mr. Greene glanced sternly at them and continued down the class list. When he finished, there was the sound of three short bells, and then the voice of the principal's secretary, Ms. Simpson, came over the intercom. We heard the same words we hear every morning.

"May I have your attention for the morning announcements?"

Since it isn't a two-way system, we can't respond, and I've always found it strange that she presents this in the form of a question. It's not like we have any choice in the matter. Why not just say something like "Please give me your attention for the morning announcements"? I made a mental note to share my observation with my friends later.

Her unanswered question was followed by the principal's booming voice.

"Happy Monday, students," Mr. Lowell said. "Just a few reminders for you this morning. Tryouts for the Drama Club's spring play will be held immediately after school today and tomorrow in the auditorium. The Science Club will be meeting in room four twelve. Sixth graders, don't forget to bring in your signed permission slips for Friday's class trip to the Lakeside Historical Society. And seventh graders, as you may already know, your student representative, Parker Friedman, recently moved from Lakeside. You will need to elect a new representative. If you're interested or you want to nominate a classmate, please submit names to Ms. Simpson in the office by the end of the school day tomorrow.

"Thank you for your attention."

There was nothing in the announcements to interest me. I'm not in any clubs, I would never try out for a play, and I don't even know what a student representative is.

It turned out that I wasn't the only one. Someone in the back of the room raised his hand, a guy who I remembered had started at Lakeside in November.

Mr. Greene nodded. "Yes, David?"

"What's a student representative?" David asked. "I didn't know we had one."

Another classmate responded. "That's because Parker never did anything."

Mr. Greene frowned at the kid for speaking without raising his hand first, but then he answered David.

"In September, each grade elects a student representative who attends certain meetings with Mr. Lowell and some faculty members and acts as a link between the students, the teachers, and the administration throughout the school year. The representative can make suggestions and recommendations for changes, improvements, that sort of thing."

David raised his hand again, and Mr. Greene nodded again.

"What kind of recommendations did Parker make?"

"I'm not on that committee, so I only know what I've heard from other teachers," Mr. Greene replied. "Let me think." He cocked his head sidewise and his brow furrowed as he considered the question. "Hmm . . . well, the only thing I remember was a suggestion that the teachers assign less homework."

"Then what happened?" David asked.

"As I recall, nothing came of it."

"Did any of the other grade representatives make suggestions?"

Mr. Greene hesitated. "Hmm...yes, I heard that the eighth-grade rep asked for longer lunch periods."

"Is that going to happen?" David asked.

"Probably not."

David frowned. "Then what's the point of having student representatives?"

Just then, the bell rang. And Mr. Greene looked relieved.

chapter three

ENGLISH IS MY FAVORITE CLASS AND MS. Gonzalez is my favorite teacher, so I look forward to third period. Plus, it's the only class that Ellie, Alyssa, Kiara, and I have together. As usual, I hurried to get there early so we could have a minute or two to talk before we had to be inside the room. And while it was still on my mind, I wanted to share my thoughts about Ms. Simpson's morning announcements question.

The three of them were just gathering outside the door when I arrived, and right away I noticed Ellie's glum expression. So instead of bringing up

Ms. Simpson, the first thing out of my mouth was "What's wrong, Ellie?"

Ellie let out a groan. "I was twenty minutes late for school and I had to report to Mr. Lowell's office," she said. "So now I've got detention."

Kiara frowned in the way she always does when anyone says anything that she thinks doesn't make sense. "You know how long it takes you to walk to school. And you wear a watch. So why were you late?"

"I went up to the turret to take a quick look through the spyglass."

"See anything?" Alyssa asked.

Just then I spotted Ms. Gonzalez hurrying down the hall, which meant the bell was about to ring. We'd have to wait till lunch to hear what Ellie saw. And for me to bring up Ms. Simpson.

I realized that since Ellie had detention, she'd be staying after school and we wouldn't have a spyglass session. I was disappointed. We hadn't had any interesting visions lately, and I'd been hoping this could be the day that would end the dry spell.

After taking roll, Ms. Gonzalez glanced at her planner and called on Aiden Panchuk.

"Your turn to kick off our book discussion today, Aiden. Are you prepared to give your free-choice oral report?"

"Yep." Aiden came to the front of the room and

opened his notebook. "My report is on *The Lion, the Witch and the Wardrobe* by C. S. Lewis."

Of course, I would never say this out loud in class, but I'd read that book ages and ages ago, along with the entire Narnia series, so I knew what was coming. Aiden started off by summarizing the story, about four children who go to live in the English countryside during World War II. Behind the doors of an enormous wardrobe, they find a land called Narnia. This magical place has been enchanted by the evil White Witch, so Narnia is in a perpetual winter. One of the children, Edmund, has an encounter with the White Witch, who gives him candy, and he doesn't tell his siblings about this. Not warning them has consequences, and the kids fall into a dangerous situation.

Since Ms. Gonzalez is into lots of discussion, we were allowed to ask questions or offer comments even during the reports. Dana, a girl in the front of the room, raised her hand.

"He lied to his own brother and sisters?" she asked.

"It wasn't really a lie," Aiden said. "He just didn't tell them about what happened to him."

"That's still a lie," Dana insisted. She turned to Ms. Gonzalez. "Isn't it?"

"That's an interesting question," Ms. Gonzalez said. "I think we could say that this was a lie of omission."

I wasn't sure what that meant and it seemed others didn't know either, because a lot of people looked puzzled and Ms. Gonzalez noticed this. She explained.

"A lie of omission happens when someone leaves out information and thus hides the truth, or when someone doesn't include a fact because the person they're giving information to wouldn't like it. Let me think of an example." She paused for a moment and then went on.

"Let's say you're in the market for a laptop. The salesperson shows you one and tells you it's a very good product with many advantages. He tells you it's easy to use, and the screen has excellent resolution, and it's even on sale. And this is all true. But he doesn't tell you that this particular brand of laptop has an unusually short battery life."

"What if you ask him about the battery life and he tells you it's good?" Aiden asked.

"Then he's lying," Ms. Gonzalez replied. "But if you didn't ask, and he doesn't offer the information, then it's a lie of omission. He didn't mention it because he wants you to buy the laptop."

I nodded to show that I understood, and so did some of my classmates.

"Can anyone else offer an example?" Mrs. Gonzalez asked.

Another hand shot up.

"Alberto?"

"This actually happened to me last summer! I was supposed to go on a picnic with some friends. One of them said he would check the forecast, and he told us it would be a warm day. But he didn't tell us it was supposed to rain."

"Why did he do that?" someone asked.

"Because he'd gotten grounded and he couldn't go. So he was in a bad mood and he wanted the picnic to be ruined for the rest of us!"

"Nice friend," I heard Alyssa mutter.

Ellie offered an example too. "I was shopping with my mother, and she tried on a dress. She asked me if I thought the dress was pretty and if it was a nice color on her. I told her it was definitely pretty and a good color for her. But I didn't tell her it looked too tight in the back."

"And why didn't you tell her this?" Ms. Gonzalez asked.

"She didn't ask me if it looked tight, and I didn't want to hurt her feelings."

Ms. Gonzalez looked pleased. "These are all good examples, and you can see that people tell lies of omission for many different reasons. To be kind, to be mean, to get out of doing or saying something. And in Edmund's case, he didn't tell the others about the witch because he wanted more candy!"

Now everyone was nodding, and Ms. Gonzalez indicated to Aiden that he could continue his report. I wasn't really listening, though. The discussion had given me an idea, and I was thinking about what it could mean for me.

After English, I had pre-algebra, and I couldn't daydream in there. But when the bell rang it was lunchtime, and I knew that could be an opportunity to talk about my new idea with my friends.

By now, we've developed a routine. I'm always the first at the table, since I bring my lunch from home. Mami prepares my lunches for the next day every evening. Like Mom, she's into healthy eating, but she also enjoys eating *good* food. So my lunches are organic and nutritious. And usually delicious.

The other girls had to stand in line to get their school lunch trays, and I waited to open my brown bag till they'd all arrived. Today, I had a cold whole-wheat noodle and tuna salad, and they all looked at it longingly. I offered them bites. In return, they offered me bits of the brownies they had on their school lunch trays. They know I love chocolate.

Once everyone was settled and eating, I was all set to bring up my ideas. But before I could get a word out, Kiara turned to Ellie and asked, "So? Did you see anything interesting in the spyglass this morning?"

"Nothing worth getting detention for," Ellie said.

"At first, I thought there was something that might be weird—about eight dogs in a circle around a tree, and I thought they might start doing strange stuff, like climbing the tree or dancing. But then this man came out from behind the tree, and I realized the dogs were with him. He was just one of those professional dog walkers."

Alyssa looked even more glum than usual. "So you didn't see anything special, and we won't be seeing anything at *all* today. Not if you've got detention."

Ellie shook her head. "The detention session is tomorrow. Apparently Mr. Lowell orders it a day in advance, so students can tell their parents they won't be home at the usual time."

That made sense to me. "So they won't worry."

"And so the parents know their kid screwed up and they can inflict their own form of punishment," Ellie said with a sigh.

Alyssa considered this. "But most parents work outside the home, so they probably wouldn't even notice if their kid came home late."

"Maybe some parents call from their jobs to make sure their kids get home—" I started, but Alyssa immediately shook her head, rejecting the comment before I could even finish it.

"Not at my house," she said. "There are four of us, and we all get home at different times. Besides, my mother might be operating on someone, and my stepfather could be inspecting a building site. He wouldn't even notice the time. I could get detention and they'd never find out." She turned to Kiara. "Does your father call to see if you got home okay?"

Kiara shook her head. "We have a housekeeper. If I didn't come home on time, she'd call him."

I looked at Ellie. "Your father's law office is in your house, so he'd notice if you weren't home on time, right?"

"Maybe," Ellie replied. "But lots of times, with his door shut, he doesn't hear me come in. He could be on the phone or with a client. And sometimes he has meetings outside his office."

Then her eyebrows shot up, as if she'd just had a great idea.

"Actually, my parents might not even have to know that I got detention."

"You won't tell them?" Kiara asked. "You'd lie to them?"

Ellie considered this. "Not exactly. If they notice I'm not home at my usual time, and if they ask me why I'm late, I'll have to tell them. But if they don't notice and they don't ask..."

Alyssa finished the sentence. "It's a lie of omission!"

Ellie nodded happily. "Exactly!"

Kiara nodded too. "Yes. I think Ms. Gonzalez

would call that an appropriate example." Then she cocked her head and looked thoughtful.

"What?" Ellie asked.

"I'm just remembering when I made a lie of omission."

"About what?" I asked.

"Back in elementary school, a couple of girls in my class called me names and it really bothered me. But when my father would ask 'How's school?' I always said 'Okay.' I didn't tell him about the bullying."

"Why not?" Alyssa asked.

"I guess because I didn't want him to go see the teacher or the principal and have an altercation."

"A what?" Alyssa asked.

Kiara searched what she called her mental thesaurus for a word we'd understand. "A fuss. Anyway, maybe the girls would have been punished if I'd told the truth, but then they'd have been even meaner to me."

This made sense to me. I'd probably do the same thing if I was bullied. A lie of omission... it was definitely a very interesting concept. Which reminded me, this was the perfect time for me to bring up my own "lie of omission" idea. And while I was at it, I also remembered that I'd wanted to bring up Ms. Simpson always asking if she could have our attention when we couldn't even respond.

I took a deep breath. "Hey, I was thinking...," I began, but as I did, I realized that everyone had turned away from me and no one was listening. They were all looking in the same direction.

"What's going on?" I asked.

"Paige," Ellie replied. "Watch, she's going from table to table." She frowned. "Now she's at Mike's table."

Even though of course it isn't a rule, at lunchtime guys usually sit with guys and girls sit with girls. Mike Twersky, Ellie's sort-of-maybe-someday boy-friend, always sits with the same group of popular boys at the other end of our row of tables. And just as Ellie said, Paige was standing by their table, talking and smiling and tossing her head so her glossy black hair danced on her shoulders.

"Flirting," Ellie said, and her eyes narrowed.

"What's she saying?" Alyssa asked.

We soon found out. A moment later Paige had arrived at our table. This time, she didn't smile or toss her hair, she got right to the point.

"I'm running for seventh-grade student representative," she announced. "Vote for me."

She made it a demand, not even a request, and moved on quickly to the next table.

"What do student representatives do, anyway?" Alyssa asked.

I remembered the conversation from my home-room that morning. Finally, an opportunity to speak! "They're supposed to make suggestions to the teachers and the administration to improve the school and make it better for students," I told them.

"Huh. I wonder what kind of suggestions Paige would make," Ellie said.

I didn't have a clue. We ate in silence for a moment while we all considered the question. Alyssa came up with a possibility just as the bell rang to signal the end of lunch.

"Hairbands. Every girl at East Lakeside Middle School will have to wear a hairband that matches her clothes."

We all nodded. That was *exactly* the kind of brilliant idea Paige would offer.

chapter four

SO I NEVER GOT TO TALKING ABOUT MS. Simpson, or my "lie of omission" idea, at lunch, and I was a little disappointed in myself. It would have been a good opportunity for me to work on bringing things up with my friends instead of always waiting for them to start the conversation. And there wasn't an ideal moment to do this with all of them now, on the walk from school to Ellie's house. Ellie and Alyssa always walk together and talk, while Kiara and I, with shorter legs and quieter personalities, trail behind.

Then I realized, I *could* make an effort with Kiara. Kiara isn't big on starting discussions either, so with only her by my side, maybe this was a chance to bring up a subject—for me to practice saying what was on my mind, just with a smaller audience. I shifted my backpack a few times before I finally spoke.

"Isn't it strange how every morning Mr. Lowell's secretary asks 'May I have your attention for the morning's announcements?' Why does she make it a question when we can't answer?"

"We could answer," Kiara said. "We could all say yes or no."

"But what would be the point if she couldn't hear us? Why doesn't she just say 'Please give me your attention for the morning announcements'? Like, be more, more—I can't think of the word."

Kiara, of course, came up with the word immediately. "Assertive." Then she looked at me suspiciously. "Is this a grammar question?"

That pretty much killed the conversation, and we walked the rest of the way in silence.

That was actually fine with me, though. Because by the time we all reached Ellie's, I'd thought of another, more interesting subject to discuss with everyone, just as soon as we all settled down on the beanbag chairs in Ellie's turret. I didn't want to be pushy—that's not me. I just wanted to be more assertive, like Kiara had said. So before anyone started talking about anything else, I spoke.

"Why do students get detention when they break a rule?"

"It's the standard punishment, I think," Ellie said, reaching behind her to turn on a string of twinkle lights.

"But this punishment doesn't make sense," I said. "I mean, the kids have to stay after school and sit in the cafeteria for an hour. So what? They could spend that time reading or doing their homework or whatever."

"Except they can't," Alyssa told her. "I got detention once last year."

"For what?" Kiara asked.

"The teacher in my social studies class was talking about the Salem witchcraft trials and how some women who were accused of being witches were drowned. Some guy in the class suggested drowning *me*. So I suggested doing something to him."

"Did he get detention too?" Kiara asked.

"No. Because he whispered his insult and the teacher didn't hear him. I, on the other hand, responded very loudly. With really bad language."

We all nodded with understanding. Because of her goth look, Alyssa gets teased—but usually in a whisper or when a teacher can't hear. It's typical Alyssa to respond like this. She'd want everyone to know what she thought.

"Anyway," she continued, "when you're in detention, you can't read or do homework. There's a monitor in the room watching everyone. You can either spend the time writing a one-page essay about what you did wrong, or just sit there and be bored. Obviously nobody chose the writing assignment, so we sat there for an hour doing nothing. It was dumb."

I didn't think just sitting would bother *me* so much. I could easily daydream for an hour.

"Mike told me he had detention once," Ellie reported. "When the monitor wasn't looking, he stuck his earbuds in so he could listen to music on his phone. He said kids do that all the time."

"So basically," I said, "all detention does is waste everyone's time." I shook my head. "If there has to be detention, why not make it so it actually accomplishes something? Like making our school *better*." I sat up straighter in my beanbag chair. "Think about it. If you get detention for writing graffiti on a wall or whatever, then you should spend detention cleaning it up, not sitting around being bored and doing nothing. And if they won't even let us do homework, they could at least make the essay mandatory, so people have to think about what they did and why they're being punished for it. The monitor could actually *help* with that, instead of just acting like a babysitter."

"That's a notable point," Kiara said. "It's logical."

I went on. "Or how about this? Two kids get into a fistfight. So then they have to sit together and discuss why they were fighting and what else they could have done to fix whatever they were fighting about."

Alyssa and Ellie shrugged, but it wasn't negative, it was more like a "yes, maybe" shrug, and I was pleased. I'd started a conversation! Maybe I should keep going and talk about the other things I had on my mind. But I didn't want to be pushy. And besides, Ellie took over at that point.

"Let's look in the spyglass," she said. "Maybe we'll actually have some luck today."

We pulled ourselves out of our beanbag chairs and gathered around the heavy base. Ellie swiveled the narrow end of the shining brass spyglass to me. "You go first, Rachel."

Was that my reward for being assertive? If so, I accepted it. I adjusted the height of the spyglass so I could see through the eyepiece. Slowly, I moved it around town.

It was mid-March and there was no snow left on the ground, but it wasn't yet springtime, so the trees were still bare and I didn't see any flowers. It was cloudy too, so Lakeside looked pretty dull. There were cars moving and people walking around, but they weren't doing anything out of the ordinary. For one brief moment, I thought I saw a daffodil, but when I moved the magnifying wheel, it turned out to be just a crumpled yellow bag.

Alyssa went next. She surveyed the area and shook her head. "Nothing interesting."

Kiara took her turn. After only a second, she drew in her breath and exclaimed, "Outstanding!"

We crowded around her. "What?" we all cried out in excitement.

"The Lakeside Museum has an exhibit on artificial intelligence and technology!"

We stepped back.

"It's turned into a regular old telescope," Alyssa declared. "Maybe we used up all the magic."

"I'm not giving up on it yet." Ellie stepped up to the spyglass. "My turn."

"Anything?" I asked.

"Just another *dog*. What's with all the dogs lately?... Wait a minute. The season's changed! It looks like it's really spring out there now. Hey, you guys, this is a vision!"

"Is the dog with the same walker you saw this morning?" Alyssa asked.

"No! I think... oh, wow, I think it's with Rachel!"

I could feel my heart beating faster as we crowded around the spyglass again. Alyssa practically shoved Ellie aside so she could look.

"It *is* Rachel!" she exclaimed. "Rachel, you're walking a dog!"

"Let me see," I pleaded, and Alyssa turned the spyglass over to me.

And there I was, ambling through the park, a lead in my hand and an adorable little dog with straight light brown fur at the end of it. And it was definitely springtime—the sun was out, and I was wearing my favorite spring dress, light blue with a pattern of daisies.

I let Kiara take a look.

"You don't have a dog, do you?" she asked me, adjusting the focus.

"No!"

She stepped away. "So you just really want one and that's why we're seeing this."

I took her place and watched myself some more. "I don't know. I haven't really thought about it much. But I loved books about dogs when I was little. *Old Yeller, Lassie, The Incredible Journey, Because of Winn-Dixie*. And whenever I saw a dog on the street, I wanted to pet it. Of course, Mom and Mami wouldn't let me. They were afraid it might bite."

"But you never asked your parents if you could have one?" Ellie asked.

I shook my head. "I never even considered it."

"But why?"

"I guess I always assumed they'd say a dog would be too much trouble. They're both really busy, and maybe they thought I wouldn't be able to take care of it. And they wouldn't let me walk the dog, not on my own."

"Even now?" Alyssa asked. "For crying out loud, Rachel, you're twelve years old!"

I faced them. "You know how they are," I said simply. "You know about my sister. They don't want to lose me."

"Do they really think you'll be hit by a car too?" Alyssa asked.

I shrugged. "Or drown in a swimming pool. Or get kidnapped by a criminal. Or fall off a cliff."

"There are no cliffs in Lakeside," Kiara said.

I almost smiled. "That's not the point, Kiara."

"But they can't watch over you forever," Ellie declared. "Aren't they ever going to let you grow up?"

"I don't know."

They were all suddenly quiet. *They're feeling sorry for me,* I thought. I didn't like that at all.

Ellie broke the silence. "Who's hungry?"

I took one more look through the spyglass, but both the dog and I were gone, and only the real-and-current Lakeside could be seen. I followed the others out of the turret, wondering as we headed downstairs about the vision and about what we'd find in Ellie's pantry.

Back home, when I get out of school, it's usually only Mom there, so my snacks are fruit or something else natural. When I first started hanging out with the sisterhood, Ellie was worried that my super-healthy eating habits meant I wouldn't want the kind of snacks *she* liked—chips, cookies, stuff like that. Since I didn't want to offend her, I ate whatever she offered and discovered that while certain snacks might not be too good for you, they certainly can *taste* good.

Of course, Ellie's parents buy healthier foods too, and raiding the kitchen that day, we found a bowl of fruit salad and carrot sticks with a yogurt dip. While a bag of chips and cans of soda could be carried back up to the turret, these snacks required bowls and utensils, so we took it all to the dining table.

We ate and talked and were generally having a good time when we heard the front door open and a voice call out, "Anyone home?"

"In here, Dad," Ellie called back.

Ellie's father came into the dining room and beamed at us. "Hello, girls."

"Hi, Mr. Marks," we replied in unison.

He looked over the goodies on the table. "May I?"

"Help yourself," Ellie replied. "We're all stuffed."

He filled a bowl with some fruit salad. "I'll take this back to my office." He started off but then turned back.

"Oh, Ellie, before I forget. I've got another meeting downtown tomorrow that's going to last till at least five o'clock, and I'm expecting a package to be delivered around four. You'll be home to sign for it, right?"

We all looked at Ellie and watched her face fall. I could see the lump in her throat as she swallowed, hard.

"I—I can't tomorrow, Dad. I won't be home." She swallowed again. "I've got detention."

His brow furrowed. "Detention! Why?"

"I was late for school today."

Again, looking more disturbed, he asked, "Why?"

She glanced at us. Of course, since the spyglass was a secret, she couldn't tell him the real reason.

"I guess I was just dawdling."

Now Mr. Marks looked very serious. But since he was a nice person, he didn't start yelling at Ellie in front of her friends.

"We'll discuss this when your mother gets home" was all he said before leaving the dining room.

The second silence of the day fell over us, but this time all eyes were on Ellie. I could see her try to smile, but it turned into a grimace.

Alyssa looked up at the clock on the wall. It wasn't yet our usual time to leave, but she stood up. "Well, I have to pick up Ethan at the Lakeside Playhouse.

Maybe I should get there a little early and watch some of his rehearsal."

Kiara stood up too. "I've got some errands to run on Main Street."

Ellie didn't encourage us to stay. She just nodded glumly, and we all went to the rack by the door to gather our coats.

With both Alyssa and Kiara going in the opposite direction, there would be no one to walk me home. In that situation, I knew I should immediately call Mom to come pick me up.

But I didn't. This was what I'd been thinking about ever since we had that discussion in English class. What I never got a chance to bring up with the girls. A lie of omission might not have worked for Ellie, but maybe it would work for me.

We said our goodbyes. Alyssa and Kiara took off one way and I started off in the other direction.

It felt strange and sort of amazing to find myself walking alone. I wasn't nervous at all. It was still light out. There were cars moving on the street and people on the sidewalks. I felt perfectly safe, and even a little light-headed. Like I was suddenly free or something!

I couldn't help but think that part of feeling good also came from how I'd spoken up with the sisterhood. It was the first time I'd ever talked so much at one of our gatherings. They'd listened to me. And then, seeing myself in the spyglass, becoming the center of attention . . . I might not have enjoyed the sisterhood feeling sorry for me about the way my parents hovered over me, but I realized that it felt good that they were interested in what I said, like they respected me! And I definitely prefer respect to pity.

In a way, it was funny that this would make me feel good. Usually, I never want to be noticed; I'm perfectly content with being invisible. But today . . . well, to be honest, being in the spotlight had been kind of nice.

I just hoped neither Mom nor Mami would ask how I got home that day. If they did, I'd have to tell the truth, and I knew how upset they would be. But maybe they wouldn't ask. As I walked, I tried not to think about it, but it was hard. I love them both so much, I can't bear to make them sad or worried. But I had a sudden vision of myself, as an adult, with Mom and Mami still walking alongside me. Ellie's question echoed in my mind. *Would* they ever let me grow up? I needed to show them that I didn't always need their protection, that I could manage stuff on my own. But how could I, when they never gave me the opportunity?

Then I saw the dog.

It was coming toward me, this little puppy with long, straight light brown fur hanging over its eyes.

I didn't really know anything about dog breeds, but he looked awfully cute.

And exactly like the dog I'd seen myself walking in the spyglass vision.

He stopped in front of me and looked up. I knew that dogs couldn't really smile, but I couldn't help thinking that this one *was* smiling at me. He just seemed so happy to see me.

"Hi there," I said softly. I bent down to pet him gently, and that's when I saw that the dog was actually female. She didn't shrink away from me, so I kept petting her.

"Who do you belong to?" I asked. I looked around, but there was no one coming after her. She wasn't dragging a lead behind her, and she wasn't wearing a collar.

I looked at my watch. Since we'd left Ellie's earlier than usual, I didn't have to hurry to be home at my usual time. So I picked up a twig from under a tree and threw it into a nearby yard. The dog immediately went after it, took the twig in her mouth, and brought it directly back to me.

"Good girl!" I exclaimed, and threw it again, a little farther this time. Once again, she retrieved it and returned to me. I could tell she was having fun, so I kept tossing the twig and she kept chasing after it.

After fifteen minutes of playing fetch with her,

and enjoying every second, I knew I had to move on. But still, no one had appeared to claim her. I started walking and she trotted along beside me, as if that was where she was supposed to be.

And she was still there when I reached my house.

chapter five

THE DOG FOLLOWED ME UP THE STEPS TO THE porch and stopped. Wagging her tail, she looked up at me, and I looked down at her. Then I opened the door, and she trotted in without any hesitation, just as if she thought this was her home.

Mom must have heard the door, because she came out of her office.

"Hi, honey," she said automatically, but then, instead of hurrying toward me for a hug, she stood still. I knew then I wouldn't have to worry about her asking me how I got home. The cute little creature who had accompanied me grabbed all her attention.

"What's—what do you have there?"

"A dog, Mom."

"Yes, I can see that. But what's he doing here?"

"She," I corrected her.

I gathered the object of her question up in my arms.

"Be careful," Mom said.

"She won't bite," I assured her. The dog didn't resist at all—in fact, she snuggled close to me. It was the strangest sensation. I couldn't remember ever picking up a dog before, and I wondered if this action always felt so good, so natural, to everyone.

"She followed me home," I said, and immediately thought I should have said "us," so Mom wouldn't think I'd walked on my own. Fortunately, she didn't notice, and I was relieved to see that she didn't look upset at all about the dog. Just curious.

"Let me look at her," she said. I put the dog down, and she went directly to Mom, who knelt, patted her, and looked her over.

"She's probably not a stray. She's very clean, and she looks well cared for. She must belong to someone."

"There was no one with her," I said. "I waited and looked around, but no one came after her."

"Hmm. She must have run off, then. I'm surprised she's not on a leash."

I shrugged. "Maybe she was in her owner's backyard and ran out."

Mom frowned. "But she's not even wearing a collar. That's strange. Why don't you look on the online community bulletin board? I'll bet someone's already reported her missing. And I'll get her some water."

I went to my room and logged on to my laptop. As I entered the Lakeside community website, I found myself hoping no one had posted anything about a lost dog yet. And I was in luck—no one had. The only missing pet reported was a cat. Of course, if the dog had scampered out of a backyard, there was a chance that the owner hadn't yet discovered she was missing. On the other hand, it was already a half hour since I'd found her, and who knew how long she'd been wandering before that? If I had a dog like this, I'd know where she was every minute.

Mom appeared at my doorway. "I think she's hungry. Honey, could you check and see if it's okay to give a dog quinoa?"

I did a search—what dogs can eat—and found the answer quickly.

"Yes! If it's cooked and plain. It looks like we should start with just a little to make sure it agrees with her."

"Excellent!" Mom said, and disappeared. I hurried

after her and caught up as she opened the refrigerator door in the kitchen.

"Mom, let me!"

She stopped and looked at me in surprise.

"I found her, Mom. She's my responsibility."

Her brow furrowed, as if she was puzzled. Then she nodded and stepped aside, and I located the bowl of quinoa in the fridge. I found a small, shallow dish, filled it, and set it down on the floor. The dog immediately left the water she was lapping up and attacked the quinoa.

"There were no dogs reported missing on the website," I announced.

"Well, let's keep checking. And maybe I'll take pictures of her. I could make flyers to post."

"I can take the pictures, Mom. *And* make the flyers."

She smiled. "Oh. Okay, honey. Feel free to use my printer."

"Thanks."

"You know, Rachel, I'm thinking that she must be from around here somewhere. She's too clean to have traveled far or for too long. I can post the flyers around the neighborhood tomorrow."

"Or *I* could," I said. "But we can keep her tonight, can't we? If no one reports her missing on the website, of course."

"Well...we should first check with the animal shelter too, to make sure no one's called them."

That was something I was more than happy to let Mom do. She took a picture of the dog and disappeared into her office with her phone. When she came out a few minutes later, she said, "All right. I contacted them and I sent along a photo. They haven't gotten any calls, but they're on alert. And they're grateful we're willing to take her in for the moment."

"We should give her a name," I said.

"I'm sure she already has one, Rachel."

"Well, just a temporary name. Something we can call her while she's here. Like, I don't know, Sweetie or Sugar."

"We'll have to go out and get her some real dog food," Mom said. "And we can walk her together tonight."

I looked at her with interest. "You like her!"

She smiled. "I had a dog when I was young. A French poodle."

"What was her name?"

"Fifi."

The dog stopped eating for a minute and looked up at her. Then she resumed eating.

"Well, let's call her that," I said. "Fifi."

The dog looked up again and scampered toward me.

"Mom! She knows her name!"

My mother laughed. "I'm not so sure about that. Maybe she's just finished eating and she wants to play."

Fifi followed me out the back door and began exploring the yard. She sniffed around the hedge and burrowed a little in the garden. I chased after her.

"Don't dig up Mami's bulbs," I warned her. Honestly, it was almost as if she understood what I was saying! She turned away, spotted a squirrel, and chased it till it ran up the tree. She barked at it, and I was pleased to hear that it was a pretty soft bark. The neighbors wouldn't be complaining about noise.

Then she snatched up a twig and brought it to me. I smiled. "Yeah, we've played this game before, haven't we?" I threw the twig, and she ran after it and returned it. I continued to toss and she fetched, over and over again.

Mami came home, and she and Mom joined us outside.

"Oh, *que lindo cachorrito,*" Mami crooned. She was right—this was a very cute little puppy.

"Her name's Fifi," I told her.

"Fifi!" Mami repeated, and Fifi ran directly to her.

Mom looked at her watch. "We should go buy her food right now before the store closes," she said.

We piled into the car—Mami took the driver's

seat and Mom sat next to her, while Fifi and I got in the back. Along the way to Main Street, Fifi pressed her face against the window and wagged her tail nonstop.

I knew where we were headed, though I'd never been inside the shop. After Mami found a parking spot, Mom got out and held my door so I could slide out with Fifi. I cradled her in my arms as we all made our way toward the storefront.

It was warm and bright inside Pet Palace, and the man behind the counter greeted us with a smile. "That's one fine-looking dog!"

He held out a tiny dog treat, which Fifi accepted happily.

"Can you tell what breed she is?" Mom asked.

He gazed at Fifi thoughtfully. "There's definitely some terrier in her. Maybe a little spaniel. How old is she?"

"We don't know," I said. "I just found her."

He examined her more closely. "I'd guess around two. Are you taking her to the shelter?"

"No," Mom said. "We'll take care of her till we find her owner. Does she look familiar to you at all?"

He shook his head. "No, but I'm not the only shop in town. There's another, at the Mall."

"We'll check with that one too," Mom said. "For now, we need some supplies."

She went off with the man, while Mami and Fifi and I browsed. I spotted a selection of leads and collars in different colors.

"We should get one of these," I said to Mami, showing her the leads. "We'll need to walk her, and I don't want her running away from *us*."

"Good point," Mami said, and I chose one in yellow with a matching collar.

"Look," I said as we rejoined Mom and the man at the counter. "We can have her name engraved on this collar!"

Mom smiled, but she shook her head. "I don't think that's a good idea, honey. We don't know what her real name is, and you don't want to get too attached to her."

Mami agreed. "Someone must be missing her very much."

Maybe, I thought, but I couldn't bring myself to feel too sorry for whoever that person was. After all, that person wasn't missing her enough to post her loss immediately on the community message board.

We checked out and headed home. After dinner, I looked at the community board again, and there was nothing about a missing dog. As darkness fell across the neighborhood, Mami and I walked Fifi around the block.

"Do you like dogs, Mami?" I asked, as Fifi stopped to sniff a tree.

"Oh, yes. In fact, when I was a child, I wanted a dog so much!"

"Your parents wouldn't let you have one?"

Mami smiled a little sadly. "They couldn't, because of my father. Once, when they visited friends who had a dog, just for a dinner, he became violently sick and had to go to an emergency room. That's when they found out he'd developed a severe allergy to dogs."

"So you're okay with Fifi staying with us for a while?"

"More than okay, my darling. I'm happy to host her!"

Back home, I put the pillow bed we'd bought for Fifi in my room, and she settled down on it. I did my homework and then got out my diary to record the events of the day. Normally, my most interesting accounts were the visions the sisterhood saw in the spyglass. Now, finally, I had something different and maybe even more exciting to write about.

When I finished recording the tale of finding Fifi, I added something else.

No one asked me how I got home from Ellie's, and I didn't tell them I walked alone. Maybe I should feel bad about my lie of omission.

I hesitated, gripping my pen tightly. Then I wrote, *But I don't.*

I put the diary away and went out to the living room to say good night to my mothers.

"Did you check the community board again?" Mom asked.

"I did, after dinner."

"Maybe check again," Mom suggested.

I didn't want to, and maybe I wouldn't have if she hadn't asked. But she did ask, I said yes, and I can't tell a *real* lie. To my relief, there were still no reports of missing dogs. I brushed my teeth, put on my pajamas, and got into bed.

"Good night, Fifi," I said softly.

Her ears perked up. She hopped off her pillow, jumped onto my bed, and curled up beside me. And it felt so right. Like she belonged there, with me. *To* me.

chapter six

THE NEXT MORNING, I HAD TO ADMIT THAT there was a benefit to having a mother who insisted on walking me to school. Otherwise, I would have been late and I would have ended up getting detention like Ellie.

I'd had my breakfast, I was dressed and ready to leave, but I got a little distracted taking photos of Fifi on my cell phone. She was treating it like a game—every time I aimed the phone in her direction, she took off before I could get a decent shot.

"Rachel!" Mom yelled. "We should have left five minutes ago!"

I stuffed my phone in my pocket, blew a kiss at Fifi, grabbed my backpack, and ran out.

"Now, we should be looking for posters," Mom said as we walked.

"Posters?"

"Or flyers, notices. Fifi's owner might have put up signs about her. So keep your eyes open."

"Oh, sure," I said without much enthusiasm.

"Here, let's check these out," she said as we passed a bulletin board outside a drugstore. I crossed my fingers as we looked the notices over. There was nothing about a lost dog.

"Have you made up flyers?" Mom asked me when we resumed walking.

I couldn't meet her eyes. "Um, no, not yet."

"Well, for now, when you're talking to people at school, be sure to tell them about the dog," she said. "She might belong to one of them."

"But you like having Fifi around, don't you, Mom?"

She smiled. "Well, yes, of course, it's a pleasure. But I'm also thinking about some person here in Lakeside who might be missing her. Someone who might be very sad right now."

I hadn't felt much sympathy for that someone last night in Pet Palace, but this morning, as much as I hated to admit it, I knew Mom was right. "Okay, I will," I said. But considering the fact that the only classmates I ever spoke to were the other members of the sisterhood, I felt pretty safe promising to do that.

"Can I invite my friends over after school to see Fifi?" I asked.

"Of course you can!" Mom was obviously very pleased with the idea. Since she couldn't know about the secret spyglass, she never understood why we always met at Ellie's.

I saw Alyssa and Kiara in front of the school entrance when we got there. I said a quick goodbye to Mom and ran to join them. But I couldn't even get the words "Guess what" out of my mouth before Ellie appeared, looking positively devastated.

"I'm grounded!" she wailed. "For the rest of the week! Including the weekend!"

"Because of detention?" Alyssa asked.

"Yeah. Mom kept asking why I dawdled, and of course I couldn't tell her the real reason."

Kiara frowned. "So, no spyglass this week?"

"I'm not sure," Ellie said. "I had to promise I wouldn't go out, but they didn't say anything about having people come over."

Alyssa looked thoughtful. "You know, if you don't ask, and they're not home when we come, it would just be a lie of omission. . . ."

I felt sorry for Ellie, but I was getting a little impatient with her detention drama. I had something important to tell them too. I reached into my backpack for my phone. "Listen, you guys, wait till you see—"

But before I could get another word out, the warning bell rang and we were suddenly caught up in the mass of students streaming into the building. I'd have to wait to tell them about Fifi when we met before third period. Except that two hours later, when I arrived at English class, the three of them were standing with a bunch of other kids at Ms. Gonzalez's desk, where she was handing out brochures about books available for students to buy at a discount.

I admit I was feeling pretty frustrated by lunchtime, which was the next opportunity I had to share my news. At our table, while I waited impatiently for the others to show up with their lunches, I carefully slid my phone out of my pocket. We weren't actually supposed to have our phones out in school at all, but my friends needed to see this to believe it. I tapped on Photos and allowed myself a small smile at the sight of Fifi. By the time the sisterhood arrived, I was more excited than ever to tell them about her.

"You're not going to *believe* what happened in my science class this morning," Alyssa was saying as they sat down.

"WAIT!" I exclaimed. Was this the first time I'd ever interrupted any of them? It must have been, because three pairs of eyes opened wide.

I lowered my voice. "I need to tell you something important that can't wait. It's about the spyglass."

At that, Alyssa immediately shoved her lunch tray aside and leaned forward. Kiara and Ellie did too, and I lowered my voice even further. "Remember that vision we saw in the spyglass yesterday? Me, walking a dog?"

They nodded. Carefully, I extended my phone toward them so they could see the photo. "Look."

Now three mouths fell open. "It's the same dog!" Ellie exclaimed.

"Shh!" Alyssa hissed.

Unfortunately, it was too late. Ellie's voice had caught the attention of the lunchroom monitor, who was now making her way to our table.

"No cell phones in the cafeteria!" she snapped as she reached out to take it away from me. Luckily, some eighth grader chose that very moment to have some fun by throwing one of the rolls that always appeared on the trays with the cafeteria lunches. I'd never eaten one, but my friends had complained about how hard they were, like rocks. And sure enough, the monitor let out a yelp when it hit her on the arm. I was pretty sure it was an accident, but the look on her face told me she felt otherwise. She spun around and went after the culprit.

I quickly tossed my phone back in my backpack and hoped this new criminal act would make her forget mine.

"Let's return to the subject of the dog," Kiara said.

"She followed me home yesterday," I reported. "She wasn't wearing a lead or a collar, so I brought her in the house. She's so cute! I'm calling her Fifi."

"Wow. Are your mothers going to let you keep her?" Ellie asked.

"That depends on if whoever she belongs to shows up. I checked the online community board, but no one's reported a missing dog. So she's with me for now. Want to come over this afternoon and see her?"

"Yes!" Alyssa said, and Kiara echoed that.

"But I've got detention!" Ellie complained.

"I know," I said sympathetically, "and if you're grounded, you can't come any other day this week. But don't worry, you'll come see her next week." *If I still have her,* I added silently. But I immediately pushed that possibility out of my head.

Ellie and Alyssa had come to my house once, over a month ago. Kiara had never been there. I thought again about how pleased Mom and Mami would both be that I'd invited them. They knew that Ellie's family lived in this old, interesting Victorian house her parents had renovated. Kiara and her father were in that elegant apartment building, and Alyssa's father had designed the cool modern home they had. I was afraid my parents might think I was ashamed of our small house, which was absolutely not true.

All I considered was our kitchen—there would be no chips or soda to offer Alyssa and Kiara. But this was a Tuesday—perfect! Mami only had a half day at the high school on Tuesdays, and when Mom let her know I was bringing friends home, she'd whip up something amazing for an afternoon snack. Her fabulous oatmeal cookies studded with dried cranberries instead of the usual raisins? Or maybe whole-grain chips with homemade guacamole. Or a pile of fresh-cut veggies and her amazing hummus?

I was still considering the possibilities during last period when, just a few minutes before the final bell, the intercom alert sound came on and we heard Mr. Lowell's booming voice.

"This is a special announcement for all seventh graders. We have three nominations for your grade representative. Submissions are closed now, and voting will take place one week from today. Your nominees are Paige Nakamura...David Tolliver... and Rachel Levin-Lopez."

Was I still daydreaming or was something wrong with my ears? A couple of classmates turned and glanced at me with surprise on their faces. Even Mr. Clark, my science teacher, was looking at me with a puzzled expression. Then I knew I'd heard correctly. My name. As a nominee for seventh-grade representative.

The bell rang, Mr. Clark dismissed us, and everyone left their desks and headed to the door. I supposed I was in what they call a state of shock. My brain told me to get up, but my legs wouldn't move. Finally, my limbs responded, and I rose. As I passed his desk, Mr. Clark smiled at me and said, "Congratulations, Rachel."

Congratulations? Like this was something I wanted?

There were no words to describe what I was feeling. Stunned? Upset? It was beyond all that. This had to be a mistake. Or maybe it was a joke. Someone was teasing me. But who would do something like that? There was a kid in my English class who sometimes teased me about being teacher's pet. And Paige, of course—but why would she nominate me? Because she knew she could beat me? But that didn't make any sense.

And sure enough, when I went to my locker for my coat, Paige herself passed me in the hallway—and looked at me in such surprise that I knew it couldn't have been her who nominated me.

Alyssa was waiting for me outside, and I immediately saw the shock on her face. Normally, at school, she walks around with a set expression, neither smiling nor frowning or reacting to anything at all. She always tries to look like nothing affects her one way or another. But now her mouth was open, and I had never seen her eyebrows up as high as when she saw me coming.

"What was *that* all about?" she asked me.

"I—I don't know!"

Then Kiara appeared. She took in our expressions, which must have registered as very unusual, because she immediately asked, "What's happened?"

"Didn't you hear that announcement?" Alyssa demanded. "About Rachel?"

"Of course I did," Kiara replied.

"And you're not shocked?"

Kiara shook her head. "No. I already knew."

"How?" I asked. "Do you know who nominated me?"

Kiara nodded. "I did."

I stared at her in disbelief, and it took me a moment to find my voice.

"Why?"

Kiara shrugged. "Well, what you said about detention yesterday at Ellie's, that was very interesting. It made me think you might have other good ideas to improve this school. And that's what a representative is supposed to do, right?"

"Who's the other candidate?" Alyssa asked. "David something?"

"Tolliver," I said. "He's in my homeroom, and he asked Mr. Greene what student representatives did, so I guess he wants to be one."

I turned back to Kiara. I wasn't going to let her off the hook so easily. Kiara always does what she thinks is right, and usually, that's a good thing. Only this time, she'd gone too far.

"Kiara, listen... you shouldn't have done that without asking me first. I don't *want* to be the seventh-grade representative."

"Why not?"

"Because... because that's not the kind of person I am!"

Kiara frowned. "You're not the kind of person who has good ideas?"

I knew that was supposed to be a compliment, but I couldn't deal with her logic at that moment. Instead I just sighed and said, "C'mon, let's go."

Walking just behind me, Alyssa and Kiara talked,

and I didn't hear a word they were saying. All I could think about was this awful thing that had just happened to me, and what I could possibly do about it.

I wasn't angry at Kiara. We'd only known each other for less than two months, and she couldn't know just how much the idea of running in an election absolutely horrified me. It's not like we'd ever talked about anything like that. But that didn't change the fact that just thinking about it made my stomach hurt—which wasn't good, since I had been so looking forward to whatever Mami was making for our snack. So with more willpower than I'd ever thought I had, I pushed all thoughts of the nomination out of my head and conjured up an image of Fifi, which I managed to hold in my mind right up to the front door of my house.

Mom opened it as I was reaching for the knob, and before she could even greet us, Fifi came running out between her legs and stopped in front of us. Then she stood up on her hind legs and panted. It was like she was saying "I need a hug," or maybe that was just how *I* was feeling. In any case, I scooped her up in my arms, she licked my face, and it felt even better than a hug.

"Cute," Alyssa said, and she didn't sound the least bit sarcastic. And Kiara reached over and patted Fifi on the head.

Mom was laughing. "Come on in, girls," she said.

By the time we'd taken off our coats, Mami was coming out of the kitchen with a tray of mini-taco shells piled high and all the fixings to stuff them with.

"I hope you're hungry!" she sang out.

Once we were all settled at the dining room table, I asked Mom how her first day alone with Fifi had gone.

"It was fine! She stayed out of my way while I was working. Then, when she needed a walk, it was exactly at the moment I needed a break."

"So you liked having her around," I said, and Mom nodded.

"I do too," Mami said. "I'm so happy to finally have a dog."

Mom gave her a warning look. "Cecilia..."

"I know," Mami sighed. "We may not be able to keep her. But I checked the online community board today, and still no one has posted a note about her."

"I don't suppose you girls heard about any classmate at school missing a dog?" Mom asked.

We all shook our heads. Fortunately, Kiara didn't find it necessary to tell her that the only classmates we ever spoke to were each other.

"Are you kids going to make up the flyers or posters to put up around town?" Mom asked me.

I made an "mmm" sound which could mean anything.

Fifi began running around the table, pausing by each of us and looking up longingly.

"I think someone wants to play," Mom said.

We'd sufficiently stuffed ourselves at that point, so my friends and I put our coats back on and Fifi followed us out the back door. Immediately, she spotted a squirrel and tore after it. We watched as the squirrel scurried up a tree and Fifi looked up at it. The squirrel ran down the other side of the tree, and Fifi took off again.

"What do you think she'd do if she caught the squirrel?" Alyssa asked me. "Bite it?"

"No! She doesn't even want to catch it. She just likes the chase."

Kiara frowned. "How can you possibly know what she wants?"

"I just do," I replied simply. "I can feel it. We have a connection."

"You've only had her for a day," Alyssa pointed out.

I smiled. "But I feel like I've had her forever. Like, I don't know, like we just *belong* together."

"Then how are you going to feel when her owner shows up and claims her?" Alyssa asked.

My smile disappeared. "*If.* If the owner shows up."

"She's a very good-looking dog," Kiara said. "I can't believe someone isn't searching for her."

"Well, whoever that someone is, they can't be looking very hard," Alyssa declared. "They haven't posted anything online or put up lost dog notices." She looked at me seriously. "Rachel...don't put up any posters, and don't hand out flyers."

I bit my lower lip and turned to her. "Really?"

"Anyone who loses a dog like that doesn't deserve her," Alyssa stated flatly.

Of course, the same thought had already crossed my mind, but I tried to be fair. "Maybe they didn't lose her. Maybe Fifi ran away."

"Then that person couldn't have been very nice, if Fifi wanted to escape from them."

"Maybe...maybe Fifi was just feeling adventurous and wanted to explore," I said. "And then she got lost."

Alyssa rolled her eyes, which I secretly appreciated.

I fell silent for a moment and considered Alyssa's suggestion.

Kiara spoke. "But you *have* to make flyers."

"Why?" I asked.

"Didn't you just tell your mother you'd do exactly that?"

"Well...not really," I said. "She asked me if we

were going to make posters and flyers. And I didn't really answer.'"

"So she didn't say she *would,*" Alyssa told Kiara, and then turned to me. "Is your mom the type who asks you a million times to do something?"

"No."

"Then maybe she'll just think you did it."

"A lie of omission?" I asked.

And two heads bobbed in unison.

chapter seven

I HAD PUSHED THE STUDENT REPRESENTATIVE nomination out of my head so well, I made it through the rest of the afternoon without thinking about it. Having Fifi around helped a lot—she got all my attention and she chased all the bad feelings away.

But I wrote about the nomination in my diary that evening.

I can't be angry at Kiara, that's just the way she is. She doesn't understand the way I am.

I lifted the pen. Did any of my friends understand

the way I am? How could they, when I don't really understand myself? I started writing again.

And besides, what do I really have to worry about, anyway? It's not like I have any chance of being elected student rep. If there are other people, besides the sisterhood, who really don't like Paige, they'll vote for David Tolliver. He's new—I don't know anything about him, and maybe nobody else does. But he can't be as bad as Paige. So Paige will win, David will come in second. The only votes I'll get will come from my three friends. Actually, only two of them—Alyssa probably won't even bother to vote, since she always refuses to do anything at school that isn't absolutely mandatory. And since I don't want to be a student rep, losing won't be a disappointment.

I stopped and thought about this. There was still something to be afraid of, especially if the number of votes each candidate got was announced: people feeling sorry for me. Or worse—people making fun of me. Ridiculing me. Teasing me. *How does it feel to be a loser, Rachel? Why did you run when you knew you couldn't win?* I'd made it halfway through middle school practically invisible to my classmates, and in spite of the good feeling I'd had at Ellie's the day before, I wanted to keep it that way. There were much worse things than being invisible.

I'd witnessed that firsthand last year, in sixth grade, with a sort-of friend of mine, Hailey. I called her a sort-of friend because we only saw each other at school. We had three classes together, and seating assignments put us side by side in two of them, so we'd chat a little before and after classes, mostly just about school, homework, teachers, that sort of thing. We didn't have the same lunch period, and we never hung out together after school, so I can't say we knew each other very well. Still, we liked each other.

But Hailey suddenly got it in her head that she wanted to become part of the popular crowd. She started copying the way they dressed and went out of her way to compliment them on a hairstyle, shoes, a bracelet, whatever. And when they gathered in hallways between classes, she hovered at the edge of the group and tried to get in on the conversation.

I observed this, in the halls and in the classes we had together, and it was easy to see that they didn't want her around. At first, they just ignored her, but when she persisted, they weren't nice to her at all. Once, I found her crying in the restroom. She told me she'd tried to sit at their table in the cafeteria, but even though there were several empty seats, one of Paige's friends had told her they were all saved. But when lunch was over, the seats were still empty.

I tried to comfort her. I told her these girls weren't worth crying over, but I couldn't convince her. And it got worse for her—there was name-calling, and mean rumors were spread. Someone would walk by her in the cafeteria and "accidentally" spill a carton of milk on her lunch. Her clothes were hidden in the gym locker room. Finally, Hailey just stopped showing up. A teacher announced in one of our classes that she'd transferred to another school, and some girls laughed.

It was always a puzzle to me why Hailey would want to be with people who didn't want her around. It's so much easier to be alone. And I didn't mind eating by myself in the cafeteria. Of course, it's much nicer for me now, having lunch with Ellie and Alyssa and Kiara. Sometimes I worry about next year in eighth grade, when we might not have the same lunch period. But I would never do what Hailey did and try to get into a group that might not want to be friends with me.

I closed my diary and got into bed. Fifi left her pillow and joined me. And with one gentle lick to my face, she wiped away all my fears.

✦

When I arrived in homeroom Wednesday morning, Paige was passing out buttons that read I LIKE PAIGE! They were big and shiny with her name in red letters on a white background. I couldn't believe she'd gotten them made up so fast. As she walked down the rows of seats, she paused by mine and started to hand one to me. Then she said, "Oops, I don't think you want one," and pulled her hand back. Naturally, there were a few giggles. I slunk down in my seat.

But I heard her say, "I guess you don't want one either, David." I looked to see his reaction.

"You guessed right," he said. Then he looked directly at me. He grinned and rolled his eyes, even more dramatically than Alyssa does. And he added a little head shake, which gave it even more emphasis. It was like he was saying we were in this together. I supposed that was meant to make me feel better. But I didn't want to be in this at all.

Mr. Greene came into the room. He saw what Paige was doing, and his brow furrowed.

"I'm not sure that's permissible, Paige. You'll have an opportunity to talk about your campaign, but you'll need to check with the office about handing out campaign materials." Then the bell rang.

"*After* class," he added, and Paige smiled brightly in response.

I noticed she didn't nod or say yes, though, to confirm that she would ask about the rules. A lie of omission?

Mr. Greene took attendance, and then the usual announcements about practices and permission slips and club meetings were made over the intercom. When that was finished, Mr. Greene spoke again.

"I understand we have all three of the nominees for seventh-grade student representative here in this homeroom! I thought maybe you folks would like to use the rest of the period as an opportunity to tell the class what you plan to do if you're elected."

My stomach turned over. Paige's hand shot up.

"All right, Paige, you can go first, and then we'll hear from David and Rachel."

I could only hope that meant I'd go third. And maybe Paige and David would take up so much time, I wouldn't have to speak at all.

Paige strolled up to the front of the class. As much as I disliked her, I had to admit she looked awfully good in her high-waisted black jeans, short red sweater, and black-and-red-striped headband. She did her usual hair toss, flashed a smile, and began.

"Okay, everyone, you should choose me as your student representative because I have great plans for the seventh grade! First of all, I'm going to change the rules about what we can wear."

I immediately thought of what Alyssa had suggested about Paige requiring every girl to wear a headband. I covered my mouth so no one would see me smile, and Paige looked in my direction.

"Oh, I see Rachel is shocked! Well, for those of us who are more fashion-conscious, you'll be happy to hear this. You know how the administration doesn't let us wear T-shirts with slogans on them? That is so stupid! They let kids wear T-shirts with the names of sports teams, why not other words? We should be allowed to express ourselves any way we want, right?"

Her friends nodded vigorously.

"And I'm going to make some changes in gym class. Why do we have to run around and do dumb exercises like jumping jacks? And no more volleyball, please. It's boring! Also, why can't we do yoga? And we should have Pilates!"

"What's Pilates?" someone asked.

"Oh, it's this *great* type of exercise, you don't have to move all that much but it gets you *super*-toned. My mother does it and she looks *amazing*! For you people who are feeling a little weak, how about a weight lifting studio? You guys could get some muscles."

"Very interesting, Paige," Mr. Greene said. "And now—"

But Paige wasn't finished, and she acted like she hadn't heard him. "And what about improving our social life? Did you know that the eighth grade is going to start having dances, just like at the high school? They're already planning one for spring, with a DJ and everything! They're just one year older than us. Why can't we have dances too?"

This comment actually brought forth applause from some girls. The boys looked less interested.

Mr. Greene broke in. "I think that's enough, Paige. David, would you like to speak next?"

I'd never paid any attention to David Tolliver before, so even though I was nervous, I was still interested in what he had to say. I didn't know if he was in any of the cliques at school, but I was very sure he wasn't one of the popular guys. His hair was long, pulled back in a ponytail—definitely not a cool look at East Lakeside. And he didn't wear the fancy sneakers most of the boys wore—he had on hiking boots.

He walked confidently to the front of the room.

"Good morning, classmates," he said in a kind of formal way. "I am a candidate for seventh-grade student representative, and I really should be taking this opportunity to tell you about my platform."

"Your *what*?" someone yelled out.

Mr. Greene frowned at the student, but David replied smoothly.

"My principles and objectives, what I would do for you if I win this election. However, I haven't had the time to establish these concepts firmly. Since other representatives have tried to provide less homework and longer lunch periods with no success, I can tell you right now that I won't be promising that. As for the improvements I would recommend, I will need to give this more thought. Thank you."

And he went back to his seat.

Mr. Greene looked up at the clock. "There are only a few minutes left before first period, and Rachel deserves a chance to speak too. Rachel?"

I couldn't breathe. *Stall for time,* I told myself. "Yes?"

"Come on up and tell us what you'd want to do as student rep."

"Um, I'm not sure. Yet."

Mr. Greene smiled kindly. "Okay. But you and David want to be thinking about this. You three candidates will have to make presentations at the next seventh-grade assembly on Monday."

I didn't know anything about this. And the horror must have shown on my face, because a couple of people were looking at me in fear, like they thought I might throw up. Which I pretty much felt like doing.

"Rachel, David, Paige, you'll learn more about this tomorrow," Mr. Greene continued. "The candidates are invited to join a meeting with Mr. Lowell and the committee members during homeroom period, to give you an idea of what's expected of a student representative. That includes attending meetings, which take place during the homeroom period once a month."

That certainly wasn't anything to look forward to either, and my stomach continued to churn.

The awful feeling stayed with me all morning. Even thinking about Fifi couldn't raise my spirits. If I couldn't even get up in front of the homeroom class, how could I stand on a stage in front of the entire seventh grade? I could feel myself trembling, as if I was already there.

My friends were standing just outside the door when I arrived for English, but no one noticed my mood. Alyssa and Kiara were listening to Ellie talk about the detention experience and being grounded.

"Detention was no big deal, I held a book on my lap under the table and the monitor didn't even notice. At home, I didn't complain, I kept apologizing, and I swore up and down that this would never happen again. I made a banana bread, which is Dad's absolute favorite. And I walked around looking so sad that I think my parents started to feel sorry for me. So even though I'm still grounded, they said I can have friends come over. Spyglass after school today, girls!"

Alyssa and Kiara were happy, and I was pleased with the news too. But overall, I was still feeling pretty depressed. By lunchtime, I'd made a decision, and I announced it to the others at our table.

"I'm going to withdraw my name as a candidate for the student representative election."

Ellie was clearly not happy. "I don't think David Tolliver has a chance, Rachel. So it'll be a landslide for Paige. You don't want that, do you?"

I shrugged. "She'll win no matter who runs against her."

Kiara frowned. "This doesn't make sense."

"What do you mean?" Alyssa asked. "Come on, Kiara, you know she's like the number one most popular girl in seventh grade. And all school elections are popularity contests."

"But that's two things that don't make sense," Kiara insisted. "Number one. Why is a mean girl so popular? Wouldn't people like a nice person better? Number two. Why wouldn't people vote for the person who could do the best job?"

Ellie had answers. "First of all, mean girls are popular because everyone is afraid of them."

"It's more than that," Alyssa said. "If a person is mean to most people, but she's nice to you, that makes you special. So everyone wants to be that person's friend."

Kiara was still frowning. "It's illogical."

Alyssa nodded. "But it's middle school. That's the way things are for girls. I think it stays pretty much the same in high school. Maybe it's different in college."

"And I think it's the same for boys," Ellie added. She glanced in the direction of a table in our row and lowered her voice. "There's a guy over there at Mike's table, Thayer, who's not nice at all. I saw him once try to trip this little sixth grader. And Mike says he plays mean tricks on people all the time. But he's still in the popular crowd because people think he's cool."

"How is he cool?" Kiara asked. "What about anything you just described makes him cool? What makes any person cool, anyway?"

"No idea," Ellie replied.

Alyssa eyed her skeptically. "But you were considered cool at your old school, weren't you?"

Ellie sighed. "But I can't tell you *why*. I guess it's just a mystery."

"Anyway," I said, "I just found out that the candidates have to make a presentation at a seventh-grade assembly next week, so that's another reason for me to quit. I absolutely cannot do that."

They all know what torture it is for me even to give oral book reports in English. But Kiara continued to look bothered.

"But you'd be a better-qualified student representative than Paige or that boy. You have interesting ideas, and you care about people."

I smiled sadly. "Thanks, Kiara. But I had one good idea, about improving detention. And maybe I could come up with more ideas. But I can't picture myself in a meeting with teachers and the administration and other student representatives and actually opening my mouth! You know how shy I am."

Kiara had to know that, and she didn't argue.

"Besides, even if I did think of more ideas, and even if I wasn't so shy, I can't win! So there's no point to this. I'm going to the office after school and withdrawing my name."

Ellie shook her head. "Not today," she declared. "We've got spyglass, remember?"

I nodded. "Okay. I'll do it tomorrow."

Now that I'd made up my mind, I was able to get through the rest of the day without worrying.

On the way to Ellie's after school, Ellie got a text message. She stopped to read it, looked pleased, sent a message back, and made an announcement.

"We can only spend forty-five minutes with the spyglass today. Mike's coming over to look at birds."

Alyssa and I gave each other knowing looks. As much as Ellie insisted that Mike wasn't her boyfriend, she was always very happy when he took her up on her open invitation to bird-watch from her telescope. Ellie saw the looks, glared at us fiercely for two seconds, and then we moved on.

We didn't have a very successful spyglass session. I'd been hoping to get another glimpse of Fifi and me, maybe one that would show us playing in the snow or something. That might mean it was next winter, and that we'd still be together then. Of course, spyglass visions didn't always indicate the real future, so it might only mean that I *wanted* to be with Fifi next winter. Which I already knew.

But neither of us made an appearance. Instead, Ellie only spotted what she thought was a vision. "Ooh, it's Mr. Clark and Ms. Hannigan, together! Remember what we saw in January?"

Kiara hadn't been in the sisterhood then, so I explained it to her. "We saw the science teacher and the art teacher in the school parking lot. And suddenly, they ran into each other's arms and started dancing."

"Why?" Kiara asked.

"It was a vision, it wasn't really happening. But we decided it meant they secretly liked each other."

Ellie was still looking through the spyglass. "Well, it's not a secret anymore, because this isn't a vision." She let us all look. Sure enough, it was an ordinary March day, and Mr. Clark and Ms. Hannigan were walking arm in arm. They got in a car together and drove off.

"So you see, visions can really come true," Alyssa told Kiara.

"Not all the time," Ellie said. "Remember when we saw Paige sitting alone and crying? She was *really* upset in that vision. But we still don't know anything that's happened to make her cry."

"Not yet," Alyssa pointed out. "Maybe she'll lose this election."

"Not to me," I said quietly. "Besides, she's not the type to cry over something like that. She'd just get angry and claim that someone didn't count the votes correctly."

Ellie, still looking into the eyepiece, sighed. "Well, whatever she's crying about, maybe we'll find out eventually."

After forty-five minutes of no visions, Kiara asked Ellie if she'd like us to leave now.

"So you can be alone with Mike."

She got the brief glare that Alyssa and I had received earlier.

"No! Why would I want to be alone with Mike?"

Alyssa smirked, but Ellie ignored it and continued. "It's just that he can't know about the spyglass visions. We have to act like it's a regular telescope. We'll just watch Mike look for his birds, and then we'll all go downstairs and have snacks together."

While we waited for Mike to show up, we each took one more turn at the spyglass. Ellie's father must have let Mike in, because Alyssa was still looking through the spyglass when he entered the turret.

"Are you a bird-watcher too?" Mike asked her.

Alyssa, as usual, had one of her smart-aleck responses. "No, I'm looking for dragons."

Mike grinned. "I don't think you'll find many of *them* flying over Lakeside."

"You never know," Alyssa said darkly.

Ellie shot her a look and then turned to Mike with a completely different expression. "What kind of birds are you looking for today?"

"Well, it's a little early for the spring migration," Mike said. "But the weather's been pretty mild, so I might spot a woodcock or a red-winged blackbird. Or if I'm really lucky, a yellow-bellied flycatcher."

He took his position at the spyglass—no, I had to think of it as a telescope now. But it didn't turn out to be a very successful day for him there either. He let us know what he saw—robins and sparrows—but according to him, these weren't very interesting. Turning away from the telescope, he looked at me.

"So, you're running to be our class rep?"

I froze. This always seemed to happen when someone I didn't know very well spoke to me directly. I was supposed to be working on this. But before I could find my voice, Kiara responded.

"She's dropping out."

"How come?"

I saw Ellie open her mouth and forced myself to speak first.

"Because . . . because I hadn't planned on running for student representative. Kiara nominated me."

"So you don't want the job?"

This time, Alyssa beat me to a response. "It doesn't matter, she can't beat Paige."

Mike didn't question this. "Yeah, you're probably right. No offense, Rachel."

I managed a smile. "None taken. But there's still David Tolliver."

"Do you know him?" Ellie asked Mike.

"Not really. He's new at Lakeside this year, like you, but he came in the fall. He kind of keeps to himself. Some of the guys think he's strange."

"Why?" I asked.

"Mostly because of the way he dresses, I think.

And because he talks like an adult. Big words and all that."

"There is nothing wrong with having an impressive vocabulary," Kiara said sternly.

"Yeah, okay, but most kids think it's weird," Mike replied. "No offense."

Alyssa eyed him seriously. "You know Paige pretty well, right? No offense to *you,* Mike, but don't you hang out with the same people?"

I had to smile at that—Alyssa saying "no offense," as if Mike should consider it a possible offense to be accused of hanging out with that crowd.

Mike shrugged. "Yeah, I guess."

"Do you think she'd do a good job as student rep for the seventh grade?"

"Not really."

We were all looking at him now, so he must have known we expected more from him. He looked at Ellie a little nervously, but she nodded, as if to encourage him to share his thoughts.

"The thing about Paige is...she'll do something if she *wants* to do it. But not if it's something someone else wants."

Kiara, naturally, wanted specifics. "For example?"

"Well, like...you know Jim Berger?"

We nodded. "He's in our English class," Alyssa said.

"And my homeroom," Kiara added.

"Well, he's a friend of mine," Mike said. "Back in September, he wanted to start a chess club. Something official, so the group could use a classroom to play games after school. He passed around a petition for signatures that he could present to the administration, and Paige refused to sign it."

"Why?" I asked.

"She told him chess clubs were for nerds and she didn't want her name connected to nerds."

I gasped. "What a terrible thing to say! What did Jim do?"

Mike actually grinned. "He told me later that he wasn't surprised and he didn't care. Honestly, she'd probably say the same thing to me if I told her I wanted to start a bird-watching club."

Alyssa wasn't smiling. "But you'd still vote for her, right? Because she's popular and you run in the same crowd."

Mike's grin disappeared, and now he looked really uncomfortable. And Ellie looked nervous. I figured she was afraid Alyssa was going to continue to challenge him and start an argument, so she quickly changed the subject.

"Has anyone noticed how bad a social studies teacher Ms. Koster is? She is so boring! She'll assign a chapter in the textbook, and the next day she practically repeats it out loud word for word. We don't learn anything except what's in the book."

"Someone should tell her," Kiara said.

Alyssa rolled her eyes. "Right. 'Hey, Ms. Koster, you're boring.' We should have student evaluations like they do in high school."

"What kind of evaluations?" I asked.

"It started a couple of years ago, when my stepbrother Josh was first elected to the student council. At the end of the year, everyone in each class gets a form to fill out, and they answer questions about the teaching, the homework, and what they think about everything. Then the teachers get the forms, and maybe they'll change stuff about their classes based on the feedback. And since the students don't put their names on the forms, they're really free to say whatever they think."

"Too bad we can't do that," Ellie commented. "Maybe Ms. Koster has no idea how boring she is." She stood up. "Hey, who's hungry? I made banana bread yesterday and my father said it was more like a cake."

Everyone headed for the stairs, but I hung back for a minute. I wanted one more peek into the spyglass, just another chance to see Fifi.

She wasn't there. But I did catch a vision. It was in front of East Lakeside Middle School. Hundreds of girls were pouring out of the building. And they all wore high-waisted black jeans, short red sweaters, and red-and-black-striped headbands.

chapter eight

I WASN'T IN A VERY GOOD MOOD THE NEXT morning.

The day didn't actually start off badly. I woke up to Fifi licking my face, which made me smile. I tossed an old stuffed teddy bear off my bed to make more room for her, but she jumped off my bed and went after it like she would chase a squirrel. When she got to the teddy bear, though, she just stood still and stared at it. It was as if she was waiting for it to run off, and when it didn't, she didn't know what to do. I started laughing, but then Mom, looking particularly anxious, appeared at my door.

"Rachel, I can't walk you to school, I'm way behind on a deadline, something I've absolutely got to finish by five o'clock."

I jumped out of bed. "That's okay, Mom, I can walk by myself."

"No, no. Mami will drop you off on her way to the high school, but you have to be ready to leave in fifteen minutes."

This meant no play time with Fifi, and no breakfast either. I hurried to get dressed. When I went downstairs to the kitchen, Mami gave me one of her precious granola bars, which I can't stand, and I stuffed it in my backpack. Then we jumped in the car.

I knew my friends wouldn't be at school when I got there, and I wasn't surprised to find there weren't any kids at *all* hanging out in front. It was too early. The only activity in the area was the arrival of teachers.

I went inside, expecting to find the building empty of students, but I was wrong. In every hall I walked down, two or three girls were busily taping posters on the walls. I recognized some of the girls, and I was pretty sure they were in the cool crowd. My suspicion was confirmed when I saw what the posters read: PAIGE NAKAMURA FOR 7TH-GRADE STUDENT REPRESENTATIVE! There was a photo of her in the center, surrounded by pink hearts. With my head down and my eyes averted, I made my way to my homeroom.

I was surprised to see that there was already one other person in the room, and it was David Tolliver. He looked up, and when he saw me, he grinned. I smiled back uncertainly. I sat down at my desk, on the other side of the room from his. Then he got up, came toward me, and sat down at the desk next to mine.

As usual, I froze, unable to even say hello, but it didn't matter. David started talking immediately.

"So, what do you think? How are we going to defeat Paige?" he asked cheerfully.

David hadn't been at East Lakeside long enough. Clearly, he didn't know the situation at this school very well.

"Nobody can defeat Paige," I told him.

"Why not?"

"Because Paige is the most popular girl in the seventh grade." Actually, I should have said the most popular *person*. I couldn't think of any boy in our grade who was as popular as she was.

He nodded. "That's what I figured. And I suppose she always gets what she wants."

I nodded.

"Well, maybe we can change that," he said.

"Do you really want to be seventh-grade rep?" I asked him.

"Not at all," he replied. "To tell the truth, I'm not

really interested in what goes on here at East Lakeside. In fact, I might be transferring out pretty soon. My folks are thinking about moving again."

Now I was puzzled. "Then why do you want to win the election?"

He shrugged. "I just don't want *her* to win it."

"Because...?"

"She has stupid ideas, for one thing. *Weight lifting?* Dances and yoga? I mean, I've got nothing against dancing or practicing yoga, but her suggestions aren't exactly realistic priorities for improving middle schools, you know?"

"What do you think the priorities are?"

He shrugged again. "Not a clue. But maybe you know what they are."

He was looking straight into my eyes, which was making me distinctly uncomfortable. I looked down at my desk.

"I'm dropping out of the race."

"Why?"

"Well, I can't win..."

"You don't know that for sure," he said.

Now I could feel my face going red. "And I'm shy," I confessed.

I still couldn't look him in the face. He had to be thinking I was totally pathetic. But when he didn't respond immediately, I glanced up.

Once again, he shrugged. And he grinned, but not in a mocking way.

"Get over it," he said.

That was when the warning bell rang and other kids began filtering in.

"Better get to my seat," David said. "Good luck." And he strolled away.

What was it Mike said the boys called him? Weird? *Yes, weird and strange,* I thought. I wouldn't call him weird or strange, though. Different, maybe. And definitely interesting.

Mr. Greene came into the room with a loud "Good morning!" Before beginning the roll call, he quickly scanned the room and said, "David, Paige, Rachel, please report to the office for your meeting."

Immediately, my heartbeat quickened. Maybe I could just tell Mr. Greene right now that I was dropping out, and then I wouldn't have to go. But he was taking attendance now, and I couldn't interrupt. David and Paige were already halfway to the door, so I got up and followed them.

There are strict rules at Lakeside about talking in the halls when classes are in session, so we walked in silence. This gave me time to consider my options. I could announce as soon as we went into the meeting that I didn't want to be a candidate. No, not *announce,* in front of the whole committee. I would go up to whoever seemed to be in charge and tell him or her quietly.

If they asked me why, I could say I didn't have time for this, that I was too busy with other things. And if they asked what I was doing that could make me so busy, what could I say? That I preferred playing with Fifi? That was ridiculous—Mr. Greene had said the committee meetings were held during school hours.

But I was being silly. I was letting my imagination run wild. They weren't going to waste time interrogating me. This wasn't a trial. They'd tell me to go back to my homeroom, that's all. And Paige would smirk, and David would look...I don't know. Disappointed in me?

In the office, Ms. Simpson directed us to a room across the hall, which turned out to be the faculty lounge. At a big table, Mr. Lowell sat at the head. Mr. Clark, the science teacher, was there too, and also Ms. Koster, the boring social studies teacher. And there was another teacher I didn't recognize, plus two students, a boy and a girl I didn't know. I figured they must be the representatives of the sixth and eighth grades.

I realized there was no way I could speak privately to Mr. Lowell. The second we walked in, he told us to have a seat, and then he got down to business.

"These are the candidates for seventh-grade representative," he said, and he introduced us each by name. Then he introduced the teachers and the other students, Sun Li and Jacob Shea. I was so nervous, their grades didn't even register at first.

"Since this is a special election to fill a vacant seat, we don't have time for a weeks-long campaign season, as we normally do every fall. The candidates will be presenting their platforms for the consideration of their fellow seventh graders at a classwide assembly this coming Monday," Mr. Lowell continued, and then he turned to us. "Until then, you're free to campaign during your lunch period, and to post or distribute campaign materials throughout the school within reason. That means posters, not balloons and confetti, and no handing out bribes." Paige, who had been examining her hands while Mr. Lowell spoke, glanced up, looking slightly disappointed.

"The assembly will take place during fifth period on Monday. As potential representatives of your peers and of this school, I'm sure it goes without saying that your presentations about how you intend to fulfill the duties of a class representative should be both thoughtful and appropriate. You will each have five minutes to speak. Kindly recall that you are asking your classmates to put their trust in you to attend our regular committee meetings and to effectively represent *them.* If you are elected, this committee will be relying on you to contribute your opinions and ideas, in addition to communicating the needs of your classmates.

"But for today"—Mr. Lowell smiled—"you are here to simply observe a typical meeting of the committee, so you'll have a firsthand idea of what to expect if elected."

So I won't be called on to present ideas, I thought. That was a relief. And when the meeting was over, I would just quietly go up to Mr. Lowell and tell him I was out. Or, if he left in a hurry or was talking to someone, I could go back across the hall and tell Ms. Simpson. It occurred to me that I could have done that when we arrived, and I mentally kicked myself.

"To begin," Mr. Lowell said, "I want to remind everyone that what we're interested in are honest concerns and practical suggestions. For example, we don't want to hear complaints about homework. Or a recommendation that we hire a fast-food chain to operate our cafeteria. But creative, realistic ideas are always welcome. We will present your ideas to the faculty, and then, if the faculty approves and the ideas require additional funding or a major change in regulations, we'll submit them to the county board of education."

Heads bobbed up and down, mine included. Mr. Lowell made it sound like this was actually an important committee. But then I remembered what Mr. Greene had told us about previous student recommendations and how ineffective they'd been.

Mr. Lowell turned to the boy. "Jacob? Does the eighth grade have any interesting concerns you'd like to discuss?"

"Yes," Jacob said. "It's about the spring dance. Instead of having it in the gym, can we hold it in someplace fancier? Like a hotel?"

Mr. Lowell smiled pleasantly. "No."

"Why not? Lakeside High has its senior prom in a hotel."

"Lakeside High has a much bigger budget for social activities than we have, Jacob. Besides, what's wrong with the gym?"

"It's boring," Jacob replied. "It's not special. We see it practically every day. It doesn't feel like a party space."

"Then decorate it," Mr. Lowell suggested. "I think we can come up with the money for some crepe paper and balloons. Anything else?"

"Can we hire a professional DJ for the music?" the boy asked.

"What does a professional DJ cost?"

"Two hundred dollars an hour. And our dance is

supposed to be three and a half hours. So that would be..." He hesitated. Clearly not a math wizard.

"Seven hundred dollars," Mr. Lowell said, and he shook his head. "I'm sorry, Jacob, that's just too expensive. Besides, can't you all just make up a playlist on one of your phones? We can hook it up to a loudspeaker."

Jacob frowned, but he shrugged his shoulders. "Yeah, okay."

"Anything else?"

Jacob shook his head.

I was surprised. It seemed to me that eighth graders would have more concerns than that. They'd be going to the high school in September. Wouldn't they like to have guided tours of the much bigger school, or maybe invite a counselor to talk to them about the courses they'd be taking there? It seemed that Mr. Greene's description of what went on at these meetings was pretty accurate.

Mr. Lowell turned to the girl. "Sun, what do you have for us?"

The sixth-grade girl opened a folder and began to speak.

"I have two items to bring up. A lot of sixth graders, most of them in fact, have laptops at home. And it's true that some students mainly use them for social media or games or streaming movies. But practically everyone also uses them for homework purposes, for research and writing reports. Only, there are students who come from families who don't have personal computers, usually because they're very expensive. So I would like to suggest that East Lakeside purchase a number of laptops that could be checked out by students to use at home."

The teacher whose name I hadn't caught nodded. "I like this idea."

Ms. Koster, the boring social studies teacher, frowned. "How would we know they're not just using them for playing games?"

"I don't know," the girl said. "Maybe there's a way to block games."

Mr. Clark shook his head. "I think that if we ask students to sign a guarantee that they will use the laptops for schoolwork, that will be sufficient. Sure, there are some who won't honor this agreement, but I think the majority of students here are honest."

"I agree," Mr. Lowell declared. "Would you please send me a copy of your proposal, Sun? I'm going to talk to the media specialist and see if we can use some of their budget for this idea."

Jacob broke in. "Hey, laptops are more expensive than a DJ!"

Mr. Lowell looked at him through narrowed eyes.

"They are also more important. Thank you, Sun. Anything else?"

"Some of my classmates want to know if there's any way we can have the media center open on weekends," she said.

"Hmm. Now, that's a tough one," Mr. Lowell said. "We'd have to hire media specialists to work there. And there's the question of additional building insurance, which is very expensive. I'll look into it, but to be honest, Sun, I don't think it's possible given the school budget. Still, it's a good suggestion, and I could bring it up to the board of education as something they could consider for all the schools in the county."

"Thank you," Sun said. "That's all from the sixth grade."

This time, I was surprised and impressed. These were really good ideas. I gazed at Sun in awe. How could a sixth grader be so sure of herself, to speak like that in front of people? I looked across the table at David. His eyes met mine, his eyebrows shot up, he glanced at the sixth grader, and he nodded at me. He was clearly impressed with her too.

Paige was sitting next to me, and her head was down. Lowering my gaze, I saw that under the table, she was filing her fingernails.

"Well, if that's all for today, do the candidates have any questions about this process?" Mr. Lowell asked.

Paige's head came up, and so did one of her hands.

"Yes, Paige?"

"I'd like to make a suggestion," she said.

Oh, no, I thought. Pilates or T-shirts? But Paige didn't get the opportunity to bring up either.

Mr. Lowell smiled but shook his head. "I'm sorry, Paige, only elected representatives can make suggestions. Do you all understand the process?"

We nodded and the meeting was adjourned. But when I got outside the faculty lounge, I wanted very much to compliment the sixth grader, Sun Li. And since the end of homeroom bell was ringing, it was okay to speak.

"Those were really great suggestions," I told her.

"Thank you," she said. "I hope that first one gets approved in the next faculty meeting."

"I was wondering, though...," I began, and then caught myself. I wasn't a rep, and I wasn't even going to be a candidate, so I shouldn't say anything.

But Sun looked interested. "What? Tell me!"

I looked around furtively, but the others had moved on, so I told her. "For families who don't have PCs, who can't afford them, well, maybe they can't afford an internet connection in their homes either."

Sun's eyebrows shot up. "Wow, I didn't even think about that! You're absolutely right. I'll start doing some research on that tonight. I'm going to amend my proposal to suggest including funds for internet connections. Or more hotspots, at least. Or *something.*"

"But I guess you'll have to wait till the next meeting to share this."

She shook her head. "We have a committee email group. I can send out the idea today."

I was even more impressed. "Wow, you can really do this? Make something actually happen?"

She nodded. "Of course, all the suggestions don't come to pass. But there's a good chance, if the idea is realistic and there's the money to support it." She looked up at the clock. "Hey, we've got to get to first period. Listen, I hope you win! I think you'd be a great addition to the committee."

I spent the rest of the morning thinking about what Sun had said.

Later, when I saw my friends in the hall before English class, Ellie told us we couldn't do a spyglass session that afternoon.

"My father asked me to help him organize his law books in his office. And I'm still trying to be Little Miss Perfect. I'm hoping maybe they'll release me from home for the weekend."

"I have more errands to do this afternoon, anyway," Kiara said. "Our neighbor broke her leg last week and she's on crutches. I told her I'd get groceries for her today. And Rachel, I assume you want to go to the office and drop out of the representative competition."

I didn't address Kiara's last comment, because I had a question of my own. "Will your family's housekeeper go with you when you run errands?" I asked.

"No, she'll be making dinner."

"So...you'll be running errands by yourself. On your own."

"Of course."

"And I have to babysit Ethan this afternoon," Alyssa said. She looked at me as she added, "By myself. On my own."

They weren't poking fun at me, just pointing out how most kids our age didn't require adult supervision at all times. Once again, I couldn't help being a little jealous of their freedom.

"Okay, okay, I get it," I said. "Well, I'll be happy to go home and have more Fifi time." Now *they* could be a little jealous.

In English, it was Jim Berger's turn to do an oral book report. He'd read a classic, *Animal Farm* by George Orwell. I'd read it last year, and I didn't really care for it very much. Usually, I like books about animals, but most of the animals in this book were pretty awful. In *Animal Farm,* some pigs take over and run the farmer off the land. At first, it's okay, with all the animals being equal and taking care of things, but then there's a struggle for power and one pig, Napoleon, takes over and starts making all the decisions for the animals.

"Napoleon changes the farm motto from 'All animals are equal' to 'All animals are equal, but some animals are more equal than others,'" Jim explained. "He gets the other animals to pledge their loyalty to him and they do everything he tells them to do. And he ends up becoming this terrible tyrant."

A hand went up.

"Yes, Alyssa?" Ms. Gonzalez said.

"I don't get it," Alyssa said. "If he's so mean, why do the animals follow Napoleon? How did he get to be so powerful?"

"Do you have any thoughts about that, Jim?" Ms. Gonzalez asked him. "How did Napoleon take power?"

"I think the other animals just *gave* him the power," Jim said. "They wanted a leader and he was acting bossy. That was just his personality. Some of the animals wanted to be close to the power, I guess so they could feel safe. The others, well, they just followed."

Another kid spoke up. "I don't think this sounds very realistic. Animals obviously don't act like that."

"Well, I think it's what they call a...a..." Jim turned to Ms. Gonzalez for help.

"An allegory," Ms. Gonzalez said. "It's a symbolic narrative. Orwell's story was his representation of what had happened in the Russian Revolution, how it began with certain ideals that became corrupt under a dictator."

Jim nodded. "I kind of got the idea he was also saying that this could happen whenever people give all the power to someone who doesn't necessarily have the qualities to lead. This is why it's better to have a democracy, where people who want to be leader have to tell us what they stand for—they present a platform. And the people can vote for the person they think will do the best job."

This was a lot to absorb. When I'd read *Animal Farm,* I thought it was just about some creepy animals. But what Jim had said made a lot of sense to me. And the more I thought about it, the more I realized what it really meant. And I wasn't thinking about the Russian Revolution.

I was still pondering this at lunch, so I spoke even less than usual. I could have talked about *Animal Farm* with the sisterhood, since they'd been in the class with me and heard Jim's report. But for some reason, the thoughts I was having—I kind of wanted to keep them to myself. Besides, Alyssa held the others' attention as she regaled them with tales of her latest battle with her mother. Apparently, Dr. Khatri hadn't been a fan of the spiderweb hoodie that Alyssa had put on yesterday morning and had returned from work that evening after stopping to shop for an alternative.

"She came home from the mall with a sweater for me. A *pink* sweater. Pink! Like I would ever in a million years be caught wearing pink! No offense, Rachel."

I wasn't really listening until I heard my name. "What?"

"About wearing pink. I didn't mean to insult you."

I realized I was wearing a pink hoodie. "No problem."

Just then, a Paige look-alike in high-waisted jeans and a headband that matched her sweater stopped at our table. She was carrying a basket and handing out candy bars. Tossing four wrapped bars on our table, she chirped, "A vote for Paige is a vote for chocolate!"

Alyssa's eyes narrowed. "What's that supposed to mean?"

"If Paige is elected, there will be something chocolate on our lunch trays every day!"

Ellie was clearly skeptical. "Do you honestly think Paige can control what happens in the cafeteria?"

The girl smiled smugly. "Paige can do anything she wants."

The girl drifted over to the next table, and Kiara turned to me.

"Too bad you're dropping out of the competition. Because you could be handing out something. Not chocolate, of course. Something healthy. Whole-wheat bread?"

"Mr. Lowell told us we couldn't hand out bribes."

Ellie's eyes widened. "Then why don't you go and report Paige for breaking the rule?"

"I'm not a tattletale," I murmured.

Ellie continued. "But maybe she'd get tossed out of competition and that David kid would win." She grinned. "Hey, maybe *you* could win if you don't drop out."

I didn't say anything, and now all three were looking at me.

"You're still dropping out, aren't you?" Alyssa asked.

"Maybe she's changed her mind," Ellie said excitedly. "Hey, we could start making posters for you!"

"No thanks," I replied. "I have another idea."

I don't know how I found the nerve. It wasn't just David saying "Get over it." But that helped. And what Sun had said...

I've always accepted being shy, and I've never

really thought about it much. It's just the way I am, like having blue eyes and blond hair. Once, I tried to write a poem in my diary. It began "Why am I shy?" It sounded like a good line for a poem. But then I couldn't think of another line. There was no explanation.

I stood up and took a notebook and pen from my backpack.

"Where are you going?" Ellie asked, but I didn't answer her. I walked down the row of tables until I came to one where I saw seventh graders, people I recognized from classes but had never spoken to before.

"Excuse me," I began, but they kept talking to each other. Because they didn't want to hear anything I had to say? Was that one of the reasons I was so shy—because I didn't think I had anything to say that was worth hearing?

And then I realized I'd spoken in a whisper, and they hadn't even heard me.

"Excuse me," I said more loudly.

They all turned to look at me. I could feel the usual freeze creeping up on me, but I fought it back.

"I'm Rachel Levin-Lopez and I'm a candidate for seventh-grade representative. I want to ask you about extracurricular activities here at school. Would any of you be interested in more clubs? Like...like a chess club? Or bird-watching?"

They actually seemed to be thinking about it. Then one girl said, "How about a cooking club? Where we could share recipes and try different food?"

Another girl nodded with enthusiasm. "We could meet here. Maybe they'd let us use the stuff in the cafeteria kitchen."

"Okay." I jotted this down in my notebook. "Thank you."

I moved on to another table and repeated the same introduction and question. This group had ideas too—a book club. A film club. A creative writing club.

I wrote these down rapidly. Our lunchtime was almost up, so I couldn't hit any more tables, and I hadn't even eaten my own lunch. I didn't care.

I went back to my table, where the others were gathering their stuff to leave.

"What are you doing?" Ellie asked. "Rachel, are you campaigning?"

I considered this. "Maybe." And then I said, "Yes. And I've got a platform.

chapter nine

IN NEXT-TO-LAST PERIOD, THE TEACHER WAS absent so we had a substitute. She was one of those last-minute teacher replacements and she had no lesson plan, so she gave us the option of doing homework in the room or going to the media center. I chose the media center, because I wanted to look for a book on training dogs. But once I was in there, I remembered something I hadn't had time to do at home that morning.

I sat down in a computer cubicle and logged onto the Lakeside community site. Scrolling down, I clicked on *Lost and Found*. There was a wallet, and a bracelet...and then my heart sank.

Lost: miniature brown terrier. Answers to Rocko. If found, please contact the Henderson family. This was followed by a phone number, an email, and a street address. An address not far from where I'd found Fifi.

I tried to stay calm. This didn't have to mean Fifi. Terriers weren't unusual—there could be hundreds of them in Lakeside. Well, maybe not hundreds, but a bunch of them. I tried very hard to think of other dogs I'd seen around town that would fit this description. I couldn't remember any, but there had to be some. The announcement made it sound like the lost dog was some kind of purebred terrier, though it didn't specify a breed. I reminded myself that the pet shop man had said Fifi was mixed-breed, maybe with some terrier, some spaniel too. And okay, Fifi was small, but I wouldn't call her miniature. The missing dog in the announcement—it wasn't Fifi.

But I wasn't able to convince myself of that. My eyes were burning, and I could feel the tears welling up. I could write the Hendersons an email, right here and now, but I couldn't, I just couldn't.

I suddenly became aware of the librarian looking at me in concern. I forced a smile, turned off the computer, and walked out.

I stopped in a restroom to dry my eyes and splash water on my face. Even in here, there was a poster for Paige. But I didn't care about the stupid election anymore. Nothing else mattered. Only Fifi.

I went on to my next class, but I couldn't concentrate. I couldn't do anything. I just stared into space and fought back more tears.

How long had I had Fifi? Only a few days, but it felt like forever. Like she'd always been a part of my life and she always would be.

When the last bell finally rang, I moved as fast as I could. I didn't even go to my locker for my coat. I knew my friends were all heading off in different directions, and I didn't want to run into any of them outside.

I hurried home. It was cold without my coat, but I was walking so fast I didn't feel it. When I finally arrived, Fifi greeted me at the door with a look of urgency.

I went in and picked up her leash and a poop bag. Then I stopped at the open door of my mother's office, where she was bent over her computer keyboard and typing furiously.

"Mom?"

She turned. "Oh, honey, I didn't hear you come in. You didn't go to Ellie's? How did you get home?"

"I got a lift with a friend."

It was a lie—a real lie, not a lie of omission—but I didn't care.

"Mom, did you take Fifi out?"

She gasped. "Oh! I was working so hard to meet this deadline, I forgot. I'll take a break, we can go now." But her eyes went back to the screen.

"No, you keep working," I said. "I'll take her out."

Mom's eyes widened. "Alone? No, just wait and—"

I didn't want to argue, but I interrupted her. "Mom! I won't cross any streets, we won't go far, and I'm taking her on my own."

She looked shocked, too shocked to speak, and I didn't wait for her to recover. I attached Fifi's lead and took her outside.

Fifi took care of her needs immediately. I cleaned up after her and dropped the bag in the trash can on the corner. And then I turned us in the direction of the address that was now burned in my mind. As I walked, I could almost hear Alyssa's voice. *Forget about it, Rachel. Pretend you never saw the announcement.*

I wished I could. I loved Fifi so much. But someone else loved her too, someone who had her before I did. I wasn't perfect—after all, I'd just lied to my mother. But this was different. There was no way I could pretend I didn't know that Fifi belonged to someone else.

I probably should have called this Henderson

family first. I didn't even know if anyone would be home. Maybe if no one answered the door, I'd have Fifi for another night. But when I reached the address, the curtains were open and I spotted a figure inside. There was no turning back now.

I wanted to pick Fifi up, have one last hug, let her lick my face one more time. But I had to keep moving before I completely broke down. I started up the walkway to the front door.

The door opened. A woman and a little girl came out. The woman held a lead, and attached to that lead was a miniature brown terrier.

The woman looked at me, then at Fifi, and smiled. "Oh! You saw our announcement. We found our Rocko. He'd gone into our basement and couldn't find his way out. Luckily, I had to go down there to get clothes out of the washing machine, and there he was!"

I really didn't care how they'd found their Rocko. And if only they had mentioned in the announcement that the lost dog was male, I wouldn't have had to suffer like this. But I couldn't be angry. At that moment, I was so thrilled, so relieved, that all I could do was tell them I was happy for them and lead Fifi away.

I was practically dancing all the way back home. Maybe that was why my grip on the lead might have loosened. But whatever the reason, very suddenly, Fifi pulled away from me and ran out into the street, her leash dangling from her collar. She only had eyes for the squirrel that was hopping along the other side of the road—and I only had eyes for the car that was coming!

Everything seemed like it was going in slow motion as I frantically waved my arms and made eye contact with the driver, who immediately hit the brakes. I dashed out after Fifi and scooped her up. By then, the car had stopped completely, and it didn't proceed until I was back on the sidewalk with Fifi in my arms. The driver stuck his head out the window.

"Everyone okay?"

"Yes," I managed to say. But my heart was pounding and I was shaking. I don't think I'd ever been so completely frightened in my whole life.

I couldn't put Fifi back down on the ground right away. I hugged her tightly and waited for my panic to pass. And as I waited, I thought about my mothers. This was why they were both so cautious, so worried about me being on my own. There were things out there that they just couldn't control. Maybe, for the very first time, I truly understood their fears. Because now I had someone to care for in a world of unknowns. Fifi was my responsibility, and I loved her so much. I had to protect her. Like they felt they had to protect me.

But I'm not a dog.

Fifi could never completely take care of herself.

She would always need me to watch out for her, to keep her safe, to make sure she was clean and fed. As a small child, I would have been like Fifi, needing attention all the time.

But I'm not a small child anymore. And I know how to take care of myself.

✦

I walked through the door at home and found Mom pacing the living room. When she saw me, she ran and threw her arms around me.

"Rachel, I've been so worried! Please, don't ever do that to me again!"

"Don't do what?" I asked, though I knew perfectly well what she was talking about. She let go of me and stepped back.

"Run out like that! By yourself!"

"Oh, Mom," I sighed. I bent down and freed Fifi from her leash. She didn't trot off but stayed by my side, as if she could sense that I needed her there at this moment.

"Shouldn't you be working on your project?" I asked Mom.

"How can I work when I've been so upset!"

I'd once read in a story about an unhappy character who was "wringing her hands." At the time, I couldn't imagine what that would look like, but now, watching Mom rubbing her hands, folding and unfolding them over each other, I understood the expression.

"Oh, Mom," I said again, but before I could get any further, Mami came into the house. She looked upset too as she put down her bag. Had Mom actually called her when I left?

But no, she was distressed for a different reason. "I went online to check the Lakeside community bulletin board before I left school," she told us. "Rachel, darling, I don't know how to tell you this—"

"You saw an announcement about a lost dog," I said. "A miniature brown terrier. Owned by a family with the last name Henderson."

"You saw it too?" Mami asked. "Oh, honey, we'll have to call these people."

"There's no need," I replied. "It isn't Fifi."

"How do you know that?" Mom asked.

"I just went to see the Hendersons. They've already found their dog."

Mami gasped. Mom went completely white.

"You—you went to a stranger's house? By yourself?"

"Yes, Mom. By myself. Well, with Fifi. They were outside so I didn't go into their house," I added.

That didn't seem to reassure them. Suddenly, I felt very, very tired. But I knew this was the time for a talk, and I pulled myself together.

"Mom, Mami, please sit down and listen to me."

They must have both been in a state of shock, because they actually did as they were told and sat down on the sofa. I sat on the armchair facing them. Fifi jumped into my lap and I held her close.

"I understand how you feel," I began. "You loved Leah, and she died. And you love me and you're afraid something terrible will happen to me too. But I'm not a little kid anymore. I'm twelve years old. I'm smart, and I'm sensible, and I'm careful. You have to start treating me like the person I am."

They were both staring at me, and I wasn't surprised. I'd never talked to them like this before.

"I need more independence. I need for you to let me make my own decisions. At least, some of them. I mean, I still need your advice and your opinions and all that. But I can walk to and from school on my own, to and from friends' homes on my own. I can run errands on my own, I can walk Fifi on my own. I promise you I won't do anything rash or dangerous. But you have to trust me to know what I can do by myself."

There was a moment of silence. Then Mami turned to Mom.

"She's right, Jane."

Mom was still pale, but a sad little smile crossed her face. "You're growing up," she said softly.

"I love you, I'll always love you," I said. "And I'll always need you too. But not for everything. I need to take more responsibility for myself. I was always so shy and fearful, I went along with everything you wanted. But I'm changing."

Mami was crying now. I reached into my backpack and brought out a pack of tissues. Handing them to her, I smiled. "See how responsible I am? A long time ago you told me I should always carry tissues. And I do."

Then I told them about running for seventh-grade representative. How Kiara had nominated me because she thought I'd do a good job. How I'd been talking to people more—not just my friends, but other kids too, about their hopes and ideas for our school. How I'd been standing up for myself. How I would have to make a speech in front of the entire seventh grade next week. At that, two pairs of eyes got very round. They were surprised, possibly even shocked. But I thought that maybe, just maybe, there was a tiny hint of approval in their faces. And then it was as if we all knew what to do next. We got up, came together, and put our arms around each other in a group hug.

"Well," Mom said finally. "I'd better finish my project."

"And I need to get dinner started," Mami said.

"I've got stuff to do too," I said.

"What are you doing?" Mom asked. "Homework?"

"No, other things." I smiled. "Nothing for you to worry about, Mom."

My mothers looked at each other and nodded, as if making an unspoken agreement.

"We will try, Rachel," Mom said, and she squeezed my hand. "We're so proud of you, honey."

Fifi followed me into my room. I sat down at my desk and logged in to the Lakeside community site. Fifi curled up at my feet. Before I started typing, I turned to her.

"I love you, Fifi. But I have to be a responsible person and do the right thing." I watched as the words I composed appeared on the screen.

"Have you lost a dog? I've found one." When I finished posting the announcement, I sent a group email to my friends.

"Want to help me put up flyers about Fifi tomorrow?"

I had a lot to write in my diary that evening. About changing my mind and running for seventh grade rep. About almost losing Fifi. About my talk with Mom and Mami.

I feel so strange, I wrote. *This is so not me! Something's going on in my head and I don't know why.* I stopped, and then added, *But I don't feel bad about it.*

chapter ten

IT WAS A BUSY WEEKEND. THERE WAS A LOT to do, which was maybe a good thing since it kept me occupied and I couldn't think so much about the assembly on Monday. Of course, every now and then it popped into my head, but at least I had stuff to distract me.

On Saturday, the entire sisterhood came over to my house for lunch. It seemed that Ellie's Little Miss Perfect behavior at home had paid off—she was released early from grounding. I had prepped them all beforehand with the news about my declaration of independence, and they came prepared to regale my parents with tales of their own examples of the freedom they had.

Ellie was Little Miss Perfect in this situation too. I kicked off the conversation by asking her what she usually did on Saturdays, and she casually described going to the public library by herself.

Alyssa came on a little strong and overdid her tales of independence a bit, going on and on about her parents' working long hours, how she and her older siblings were given great responsibility, how she was often left alone to babysit her little brother.

Kiara, naturally, took my request literally.

"I run errands for the woman who lives next door, and I go all over town by myself. When our housekeeper is very busy, I go out to get groceries, by myself. Almost every week, I visit my aunt at her beauty salon. By myself."

After lunch, we posted the flyer I'd made about Fifi online and printed out copies. Before we left with them, I showed one to Mom and Mami.

"Shouldn't you add a description of the dog?" Mom asked.

"Maybe a picture?" Mami suggested.

I shook my head. "If I did that, anyone who wanted a dog could claim her. This way, if someone calls, I'll ask them to describe their lost dog and I'll be able to tell if they might be talking about Fifi."

I could tell my mothers were impressed by my thinking. Maybe even a little surprised.

I picked up a roll of tape, and we went out to distribute the flyers, starting along Main Street. A couple of stores let us put one up in their window, but some wouldn't. After about half an hour, we found ourselves admiring the window display at Tinsel, a very cool clothes shop. I couldn't take my eyes off a cropped pink sweater with gold threads running through it.

"Why don't you go try it on," Ellie suggested. "It'll look even better on you than on the mannequin." We went in and I located the pink sweater hanging on a nearby rack. But even before I began to search for my size, I spotted the price tag on a tiny card perched above the display. Two hundred dollars for a thin sweater? Was that real gold on it?

So I didn't bother taking it into the dressing room. We spent a few more minutes poking around, though, and while we did, Ellie asked a salesperson if we could put the flyer in their window. She took one look at us and must have figured we weren't potential customers—not that day, and probably not ever—because the answer was no.

We pressed on. We put flyers on bulletin boards at the library and the post office. We stuck them on benches in the park, on a construction site fence, all over town. At one point we stopped back at my house so Fifi could come along with us for a little bit, and even though I knew it was ridiculous, I kept wondering if she knew what we were doing. All I could do was hope that nobody would respond to our efforts.

On Saturday evening, I went to the movies with Mom and Mami. The movie wasn't something I particularly wanted to see, but I felt like I needed to assure them that my newly proclaimed independence didn't mean I wouldn't want to be with them occasionally. And it *did* distract me a little from thinking about Monday.

On Sunday, I did my homework in the morning after one of Mami's particularly fabulous breakfasts. And then, after lunch, I got to work on my speech for Monday.

As I wrote the words, I tried to imagine saying them out loud in front of the entire seventh grade at the assembly. But that got my heart beating too quickly and my stomach churning, so I just concentrated on writing. I didn't even want to practice it, not with my friends, not with Mom and Mami. It might sound all wrong—they might make suggestions I didn't want to hear. When I finally had it the way I wanted it, I put it in my backpack and wondered if I'd be able to sleep that night.

Miraculously, I did. Having Fifi snuggled next

to me helped. Still, on Monday morning, I was all nerves. I almost asked Mom if she wanted to walk me to school one last time, but I managed to stop myself. I had to stay strong, to hang on to my goals. Independence. Confidence.

Mami had already left for work in a flurry of "I love yous" and "Good lucks" and "Don't be lates," but I had a few extra minutes to spare at the dining room table with Mom before I headed out.

"Do you want me to give you one of my pep talks?" she asked, smiling.

I smiled too. "I don't know. A speech in front of the entire seventh grade is a little different from a book report."

"You're going to do *great,* Rachel."

I stood up to leave. "I know this isn't easy for you," I told her. "Letting me go off on my own. But deep in your hearts, you and Mami know I'm ready, right?"

I could see that her eyes were brimming, but she held back the tears. "Absolutely, darling. Just..."

"...be careful," I finished for her. "I will." And I gave her an extra-tight hug.

My friends were all in front of the school entrance when I arrived, and I got the distinct impression from the way they suddenly went silent that they'd been talking about me. I was the focus of their attention.

Ellie spoke first. "Are—are you okay?"

"Of course I'm okay," I replied. "I walked for twenty minutes by myself. It wasn't a dangerous adventure."

Alyssa did her eye roll. "We're talking about the *assembly,* not your walk. Are you ready to give a speech in front of the entire seventh grade?"

Like I hadn't been thinking about that for three days? But just hearing the words got my heart thumping and my stomach churning, and I could imagine my face going even paler than normal.

Ellie could see how tense I was. "You look good," she said encouragingly.

"Thanks." I'd made more of an effort than usual that morning. A little gel on my hair to tame the frizz. A green shirtdress with brown tights. Flats instead of sneakers. I actually own a headband that would have gone nicely with the dress, but no way—it would have looked like I was imitating Paige. I even dabbed on some lip gloss.

Ellie, being the one who can best understand people's feelings, changed the subject. "Did you get any calls about Fifi?"

That was something else I didn't really want to think about, but fortunately I could give a positive answer—well, negative grammatically, but positive for me.

"No, no one's called. But thanks for asking." I

looked at my watch. "Listen, I'm going to go to homeroom early so I can look over my speech. I'll see you all later."

"Want to practice on us?" Alyssa asked, but I pretended not to hear this and kept walking.

I wished there was some way I could skip homeroom, where I'd have to see the two other candidates. Maybe pretend I had a little stomachache and go to the nurse? But no, that would be contrary to my goals. I had to deal with this head-on, in a mature and responsible way.

Once I was in my seat, I opened a book and pretended to be engrossed in it as people came into the room. I didn't have to worry about Paige—she was immediately caught up in her usual little clique. David Tolliver did catch my eye, but all he did was grin and give me a thumbs-up.

"May I have your attention for the morning announcements?" Ms. Simpson's voice rang out over the intercom. After the usual report on meetings and practices, Mr. Lowell said, "During fifth period, the seventh grade will report to the auditorium for an assembly. The candidates for seventh-grade representative will speak. Voting will take place tomorrow in homeroom."

I really wouldn't have to fake a stomachache if I wanted to go the nurse, since I now actually had one.

But I held on, and I went through the whole morning in a fog. Lucky for me, there were no pop quizzes and I wasn't called on in any classes.

I saw the sisterhood before English class, and Ellie told us we could have a spyglass session that afternoon. It was something to look forward to if I survived the assembly, I thought. At lunch, I told them I wanted to sit alone and read over my speech. Being friends, they understood. But when the lunch period was almost over, they cornered me.

"You can do this," Ellie declared. "You're smart, you're confident, you're the best person for the job. No one is going to laugh at you."

Kiara nodded. "Because they know that if they do, they'll get into a lot of trouble."

"Well, maybe," Ellie said, "but mainly because they'll appreciate what she's saying!"

"And if you feel nervous," Alyssa said, "just picture them all naked."

"Why?" Kiara asked.

"I don't know, I just read that somewhere. That way the audience doesn't look frightening."

I drifted through fourth period, and then it was time to add a little lip gloss. As I walked into the auditorium in a line with my class, I followed the person in front of me into a row. Then, looking up at the stage, I saw Paige and David already sitting there with an empty chair between them. Where I was supposed to be.

This meant I had to go back out to the aisle, murmuring "Excuse me, excuse me" as I bumped people's knees. Then I went to the side of the stage, climbed the steps, and walked across the stage to my seat. I'm not sure how I managed this—I felt like I'd put my legs on some sort of automatic setting and they just took me to my destination without my even moving them.

Once in my seat, I automatically looked down at the floor, like I always did in class. But then I remembered my goals, and I realized that looking down would make people think I didn't want to be there, like I didn't want to be seen. I wasn't going to be invisible anymore. They'd all be looking at me when I stood at the microphone.

So I focused straight ahead instead, and immediately I wished I wore glasses. Then I could take them off and everyone would be blurry. That might have helped me feel less nervous. Too bad I had twenty-twenty vision.

Mr. Lowell came onto the stage and stood at the microphone.

"Good afternoon, folks. Today we will hear from your three candidates for seventh-grade representative. This is a very significant position. Your representative represents *you*. This person will attend meetings with faculty and administrators. The representative will be invited to present ideas and suggestions and offer opinions about what we do at East Lakeside Middle School. Your needs and desires will be communicated. As these candidates present their plans, listen carefully to how they will fulfill this role, what they will do for you, and consider your choices well."

He put a hand in his coat pocket. "I have the three names in here, and I will pick one at random to speak first." He took out a slip of paper. "Our first presenter will be Paige Nakamura."

There was clapping, and some cheers, but Mr. Lowell put up his hand.

"Please hold your applause until after each presentation."

The noise subsided, but someone still yelled out, "Go, Paige!"

With a big, bright smile on her face, Paige got up and went to the microphone. I had to admit she looked exceptionally cool today, in a short camel-colored skirt and matching ankle boots. A pink sweater with gold threads—I recognized it, the expensive sweater from the window at Tinsel! A headband, of course, the exact same camel color as her skirt and boots. But this time there was a little bow on the band, a pink knot that matched the sweater. I felt very sure that in the next few days I'd see many girls with bows on their headbands.

"Helloooo, my people," Paige said, drawing out the greeting as her smile got even bigger and brighter. "I'm *so* excited to be your next rep, and I can't wait to tell you the great ideas I've got! You're going to *love* them!"

She went on to propose all the plans she'd described back in our homeroom. Changes to the dress code, new options for gym class, to which she now added an indoor swimming pool for low-impact aerobic exercise. And dances, of course.

"We could even have a prom, like they have in high school! *Amazing* dresses for girls, tuxes for the guys, and we'll ride to school in limousines! Now, we all know that East Lakeside Middle School is the best middle school in the whole state. Vote for me to make it *better* than best!"

There was applause again, and cheers, and even some whistles. As she returned to her seat, I felt myself becoming more and more terrified. Then David whispered in my ear.

"Get over it."

And I had to, fast. Because the next name that came out of Mr. Lowell's pocket was mine.

My legs were trembling, but they got me to the microphone. I opened my notebook.

"Hello. I'm Rachel Levin-Lopez. I've been talking to some of you this past week, asking you for your ideas about what you'd like to see here at East Lakeside. Many of you would like to have more extracurricular activities, clubs where we can share common interests with other students. A cooking club, for example. A chess club, where you could play games. A club for people who are interested in bird-watching, where you could go on outings together. Clubs for discussing books or movies." Then, maybe because of Paige and her expensive pink sweater, I added something new that had just come to me.

"If you're into fashion, maybe you'd like to learn how to design your own clothes. Maybe the school could hire an instructor and get some sewing machines. I'm sure there are a lot of us who love the clothes we see in shops, but they're very expensive. Maybe we could start making our own!"

I could have sworn I heard a buzz in the audience, like people were talking about this.

"I've also thought about some complaints I've heard. Some people think certain classes are boring. Or you get assignments that don't help you to understand the subjects. We could do class evaluations, where you could list your concerns. And also write about what you like. The teachers could read them, and maybe they'd be interested in your comments.

These would be anonymous—no one would know who wrote what."

There was utter silence in the room now. At least no one was laughing.

"And finally, I'd like to recommend changes in the ways students are punished for infractions. Right now, we have detention where we're just supposed to sit around. But what does that accomplish?" I went on to describe my ideas for more productive ways we could spend that time.

"If those are the kinds of changes you'd like to see around school, then please vote for me, and we can all work together on improving East Lakeside Middle School."

And then I was finished. I'd done it. I hadn't fainted, or frozen, or thrown up.

"Thank you," I remembered to say, and went back to my seat.

There was applause—maybe not as much as Paige got, but it was real, and loud. I felt good. And I think I was smiling—not as wide or as bright as Paige smiled, but definitely a more sincere smile.

Then it was David's turn. He got up and went to the microphone.

"Hi, I'm David Tolliver. I signed up to be a candidate for seventh-grade representative. But after hearing what Rachel Levin-Lopez had to say, I've decided to withdraw my name from consideration. Because honestly, I can't come up with anything better than what she presented to you. She's got great ideas, and you need someone like her to represent you. I'm voting for her, and I hope you do too."

I heard Paige draw in her breath, but I wasn't shocked. I knew David didn't want the job. I didn't know if his dropping out, or encouraging others to vote for me, would make any difference. But it felt wonderful, what he said. To hear that I'd impressed someone, that someone actually believed in me and took me seriously. And that was all I needed.

The fog I was in before the assembly returned as soon as it was over. Or maybe I was just on a cloud. I was dimly aware of kids I barely knew who were saying nice things to me. I didn't really start coming back to reality until we arrived at Ellie's.

For once, we didn't go straight up to the turret. Ellie ordered us to sit at the dining table, and she disappeared into the kitchen.

I hadn't said much on the way home, and I must still have looked pretty dazed, because Alyssa asked if I was okay.

"I can't think of a word that can describe what I'm feeling right now," I told them.

Naturally, Kiara had several. "Ecstatic. Or maybe

enraptured. Exhilarated?" She cocked her head to one side and looked thoughtful. "All *e* words. Interesting."

"Well, they all sound good to me," I assured her.

Ellie emerged from the kitchen with a big cake on a platter.

"I made this last night, so we could celebrate," she announced. As she set it on the table, we saw my name on the chocolate-frosted top in squiggled pink icing.

We all swooned over it, but I asked, "How did you know we'd have something to celebrate? What if I'd been terrible at the assembly?"

"Oh, I knew you'd be good," Ellie assured me. Then she grinned. "Besides, if you'd been terrible, you'd have needed some comfort food. What's better than chocolate for that?"

"Not when it comes from Paige," Alyssa muttered, and we all laughed.

"You were much better than she was," Kiara told me.

"Thanks."

"But you still won't win the election," she added.

"Kiara!" Alyssa and Ellie cried out in unison.

"Well, you told me it's a popularity contest, right? And I presume Paige is still more popular than you are, Rachel."

"A lot," I agreed.

"But a lot more people know who you are now," Ellie declared.

I guessed she was right, but I didn't know how I felt about that. Maybe I wouldn't be able to hide anymore. Maybe I wouldn't be invisible anymore. It was a little scary. But maybe a little exciting too.

We ate a lot of cake and then went up to the turret. Ellie headed for the spyglass.

"I'll bet I see Rachel with a crown on her head," she said. "Queen of East Lakeside Middle School!" She positioned the spyglass so she could look through it. And then she fell silent.

"You see a vision?" Alyssa asked.

"Yeah."

"What?" we chorused.

She turned toward us, and she wasn't smiling.

"Rachel, you better come see."

She moved the eyepiece to me and I looked. I saw snow on the ground, and someone walking.

It was Paige.

Holding a lead.

And on the end of the lead was Fifi.

chapter eleven

"MAYBE IT DOESN'T MEAN ANYTHING," ALYSSA said.

"The visions always mean *something,*" Kiara told her.

They'd all had a look in the spyglass, and now our happy celebration had suddenly turned sour. Joy became despair.

Ellie tried to come up with an acceptable explanation. "Well, sometimes it shows feelings. Like, maybe Paige wants a dog. It could be a vision of next winter, when she has her dog. A dog that looks like Fifi."

I shook my head. "That *was* Fifi. And I think

the vision could be showing *last* winter. When Fifi belonged to Paige."

"You don't know that for sure," Kiara argued. "Did you ever see Paige with a dog?"

"No. But I never see Paige except at school." I got up. "I need to find out if Fifi is Paige's dog."

"No, don't!" Alyssa cried out. "Look, if Paige asks you directly if you've found her dog, okay, I guess you'll have to tell the truth. But if she doesn't ask you..."

"A lie of omission?" I shook my head. "Not this time. I have to go."

I walked home faster than normal. It wasn't because I was anxious to do this. You don't want to go to the dentist when you need to have work done, but you make the appointment for a time as soon as possible. Because you want to get it over with. I was going to lose my beloved Fifi. Maybe I could put this off for a while, but that wouldn't make it any easier. I had to do it now, quickly. And then cry for a very long time.

I opened my front door. Fifi came running to me, and Mom came out of her office.

"Hi, honey! How was school? How was your speech?"

"Fine, Mom, absolutely fine, I'll tell you about it later. There's something I have to do right away."

I went to my room, took *The East Lakeside Middle School Student Directory* from my bookshelf, and looked up Paige's address. Then I collected Fifi's lead.

"I just took her out a half hour ago," Mom told me as Fifi followed me back to the door.

My expression must have betrayed my feelings. I had to tell her about this or she'd worry.

"I think I've found Fifi's owner. I'm taking her there now."

"Who is it? Did someone call you?"

"No. I think it's a classmate." I didn't have to lie. "A friend saw her walking with Fifi a while ago."

"Oh. Where does this classmate live?"

"Hopkins Terrace."

"That's way across town! Do you want to wait till Mami comes home with the car and we can drive you? Or I could walk with you."

"No thanks, Mom. I need to do this on my own."

"Okay. Oh, honey, I'm so sorry."

"I'm okay, Mom. But I'll probably cry when I get back."

"So will I," she said.

"Our last walk, Fifi," I whispered as I fastened the lead to her collar. She looked up at me, and I thought I saw sadness in her eyes. But maybe this was just a reflection of my own sadness.

She wasn't easy to walk that afternoon. She kept

stopping, and I had to tug on the lead. It was like she knew where she was going.

Of all the people in the whole wide world, why Paige? Would she be any nicer to a dog than she was to people who weren't in her group of friends?

We finally arrived at the address. It was in the fanciest section of Lakeside, the neighborhood where Alyssa's family lived. Paige's house was as big as Alyssa's, though not as modern. It was white brick, three floors, and there were columns on either side of the door. What looked like rosebushes lined the front of the house. They were bare now, but they were probably beautiful in the summer. Would Fifi be punished if she dug in the ground around them? I wished I could see the backyard. Were there trees? Would there be squirrels for her to chase?

I went up the walkway, pressed the doorbell, and heard chimes ringing inside the house. An attractive woman with a pleasant face opened the door. She looked a little like Paige, only friendlier. From somewhere in the house, violin music was playing.

"Hello. May I help you?"

Before I could even introduce myself, she spotted Fifi. "Oh, my! Where did you find her?"

"On a street, near where I live on Patton Drive. She wasn't wearing a collar so I brought her home to my house for a few days."

"Come in, dear. What's your name?"

"Rachel Levin-Lopez."

She turned in the direction of a curved staircase. "Paige! Could you come down here, please? Have a seat, Rachel. Would you like something to drink? Lemonade, a soda?"

"No, thank you." I didn't want to sit down either. I wanted to be out of there as fast as possible, even though it meant leaving my darling Fifi behind.

A few seconds later, Paige came down the fancy stairs with a violin in her hand.

"Mom, I'm practicing!" she complained. Then, when she saw me, her eyebrows went up.

I'm pretty sure my mouth was already half-open in surprise as I realized where that pretty music had come from. "You play the violin?"

She indicated the instrument in her hand. "Well, *duh*. What are *you* doing here?"

Either of my mothers would have given me a very stern look if I'd spoken like that to anyone, but I guessed Mrs. Nakamura must be used to her daughter's rude behavior.

"She found Fluffy!" Mrs. Nakamura exclaimed.

Fluffy. Fifi could sound like Fluffy to a dog. No wonder she'd responded so quickly to her new name.

Fifi, Fluffy—whatever her name was, didn't run to

Paige like she always ran to me. She just stood there. Paige looked at the dog.

"Oh." There were no big, bright smiles, no shrieks of joy. Paige seemed to be processing all this.

"I was just wondering today why I hadn't seen her around," Mrs. Nakamura said.

I figured in a house this size, a dog could disappear for a week and people wouldn't notice.

"Why didn't you tell us she was missing?" her mother asked Paige.

"Um...I guess I forgot about her."

"Paige! How could you forget about your pet? You were supposed to be taking care of her."

"I know, I know," Paige said. "But she was getting to be such a pain. I'd be on the phone and she'd be trying to jump on my lap. And she kept getting into my bed and licking me. Yuck. And then she'd need to go outside and I wasn't in the mood for a walk. And she chewed my favorite shoes."

Her tone was upsetting me so much, I had to speak up. "Did you even bother to feed her?"

"I didn't have to. Lily did."

Who was Lily, I wondered. A sister? Probably a maid. It didn't matter. Clearly, Paige hadn't been very attentive.

Mrs. Nakamura was frowning now. "Paige, when your cousin's dog had puppies you begged us for one."

"I just thought she was cute."

Like a handbag, I thought. Or a new headband. An accessory.

Now Paige's mother looked seriously annoyed. "Paige, you do not deserve this dog. And if you can't take care of Fluffy, we should give her to someone who can."

Paige just shrugged. It was an expert "I don't care" shrug.

"All right, then." Mrs. Nakamura turned to me. "Rachel, would you like to keep Fluffy?"

Fifi, I corrected her silently. But I only said, "Yes, please."

"Shouldn't she have to pay me for the dog?" Paige asked.

Finally, Mrs. Nakamura gave her daughter the kind of look any mother would give a child who'd said something rude and horrible. "No."

A few moments and a hurried phone call from Paige's mother to Mom later, I was walking out the door with Fifi scampering by my side. I'd barely turned off the walkway when I heard a voice behind me.

"Wait a minute," Paige ordered.

I turned to see her holding a dog collar in her hand. It was a neon purple color with the name Fluffy in rhinestones on it.

"Did you make this for her?" I asked.

She gave me one of those "you're an idiot" looks, and said, "I ordered it online."

"Oh." It seemed to me that she must have cared about the dog, to buy something like this with her name on it. And I couldn't stop thinking about something else too.

"You play the violin really well," I said. "I thought it was coming from a music system."

She didn't thank me for the compliment. "Listen," she said sharply. "Don't tell anyone about that, okay?"

I was on the verge of asking "why not" when it hit me. Maybe around her crowd, playing the violin was as nerdy as playing chess.

"Okay," I replied.

"And don't tell anyone I gave you the dog."

Like it had been a gift! But I just nodded and repeated, "Okay."

And without another word, she turned and headed back into her house.

I looked at the collar in my hand. In my opinion, it was ugly. I bent down and showed it to Fifi. She turned her head. I had a feeling she'd probably hated wearing it. Maybe I could contribute it to a rummage sale someday.

"You'll never wear it again," I assured her. And as I headed for home with my new dog, I decided that this had to be the very best day of my life.

chapter twelve

Dear Diary,

I wrote a long entry last night, because a lot happened yesterday. I gave a speech for the first time in my life, I almost lost my precious Fifi, and then I found out Fifi was mine for keeps. She is now officially Fifi Levin-Lopez.

Important stuff happened today, Tuesday, too, but I don't want to just report it. I want to think about it. What does it all mean?

I started this diary on January 1. When I look back now at what I wrote then, every day sounded pretty much the same. I wrote about the grades I got on essays and tests, about books I read and TV shows I watched. I wrote about ideas for poems and stories, but I never got around to actually writing them. Pretty boring stuff.

After I met Ellie and Alyssa and Kiara, my entries became more interesting. First, because of the spyglass. I'd never experienced anything magical before, and it was very exciting seeing these visions and trying to figure out what they meant. And then there was the friendship. I'd never had that before in my life either, not really. I'd always been a loner, and I thought I would always be a loner. Because I'm different, and I didn't think I fit in with other people. But getting to know three other girls who are also different, in different ways, well, that was pretty exciting too.

Things are changing a lot for me. It seems like I'm doing or thinking something new or different every day. When I met my friends this morning before school, they already knew about Fifi. I'd texted them the minute I got home from Paige's. This was something new for me, sharing my news with people besides Mom and Mami, and knowing there were people other than Mom and Mami who were really interested in me.

Going to classes was different today. I used to keep my head down and I tried not to be noticed. And I wasn't. But today, people said hi to me, and even wanted to talk about my presentation at the assembly yesterday. I kind of knew most of them because they've been in my classes, but they were never quite real to me. They were just faces and names. (Actually, since I never looked people in the eye,

I didn't really know the faces all that well.) But some of them seemed nice.

I thought it would be weird today, seeing Paige in homeroom. Not just because it was election day. Even though more people know who I am, and my speech was better than hers, she's still the most popular girl in school, so I knew she'd win. But more because of Fifi, her old Fluffy, and what happened yesterday. I still can't believe you could have a dog like that in your life and not want to take care of her.

Paige didn't say anything to me. She just hung around with her clique like she always does, and that was fine with me. But I found myself glancing in her direction every now and then. Now, knowing that she played the violin beautifully, I felt like she had become even more of a mystery to me.

I talked to David Tolliver a little. I wanted to thank him for supporting me. Also, I'd kind of like to get to know him better. He's different too—the way he talks, and dresses, and acts. I like his differences. Too bad he's going to transfer schools. But he said it was just a possibility, so maybe he'll stay.

We voted for seventh-grade student representative after the morning announcements. We had real, official-looking ballots to fill out, and Mr. Greene told us to hold them so no one could see whose name we were checking. Then he collected them and told us he'd take them to the office after homeroom, where they'd be tallied by the end of the day.

At lunch, I sat with Ellie and Alyssa and Kiara, as usual. But this time, when people passed us, some of them said hello. Alyssa wasn't very friendly to them, and Kiara looked suspicious, but Ellie didn't mind as long as they weren't in the cool crowd. I wonder sometimes if everyone in the popular crowd is as terrible as she thinks they are. Maybe some of them are different, in good ways. Like Mike Twersky. Not that I want to become popular or anything like that. I just feel like I'm more interested in finding out about people than I used to be.

In homeroom Mr. Greene told us the winner of the election would be announced by the last period, and it was. All day I was so sure that Paige would win that I wasn't even excited at all. So when the intercom came on and Mr. Lowell's voice said, "Good afternoon, East Lakeside, and your attention, please. This is a special notice for seventh graders. The results have been tallied, and I'm pleased to announce that your new class representative is Rachel Levin-Lopez," I was stunned. I just sat there, I didn't know what to do or say. Actually, all I really had to say was "thank you" a hundred times to people who congratulated me, and that wasn't hard.

So much of my life is suddenly so different compared to what it was a short time ago. I'm becoming independent, and I honestly believe Mom and Mami are going to be okay with this. I think I'm really getting over my shyness. When I think about going to committee meetings with teachers, I get nervous, but I think I can handle it. Ellie and Alyssa and Kiara will still be my best friends, but I might get to know more people too. Like David Tolliver. And one of these days, I'm going to stop just thinking about ideas for poems and actually write one.

I'm changing, that's for sure. And as I change, I have to wonder, will I still be me? I don't think I'm a different person today than I was two months ago, for instance. I feel like I'm still me. So maybe what this all means is that I'm getting to be even more me! Does that make any sense at all?

Yes, I think it does. Because if it didn't make sense, I wouldn't be feeling this way. Like I'm becoming the person I'm meant to be.

I think I'm going to like being her.